HAREM KING

VOLUME 1

AUGUST D. HEART

Made with ♥ on the Notion Press Platform
www.notionpress.com

To Sagar Bhattarai, a true friend who offered unwavering support and encouragement throughout the writing of this novel. Your belief in me fueled my own, and I am eternally grateful.

Contents

Foreword

A Compelling Action Adventure Fantasy Drama that keeps you invested throughout the storyline.

After you finish one chapter,you can't help yourself but jump right into the next one.

If you're a fan of the genre, you won't be disappointed.

Interesting and Likeable Characters, fabulous world building and intriguing plot makes for a brilliant read.

You root for the good guys and despise the bad guys.

And trust me there are plenty to those.

What more do you need?

Still not sold?

There are Elves, Dwarfs,Demons,Saints,Fairies and even Gods who play active role in the major events that takes in this realm.

The protagonist Arthur, a nobody from our world, all of a sudden gets transported into an unknown almost Mythical World where he finds himself to be the Crown Prince of a very powerful Kingdom.

He all of a sudden finds himself to be surrounded by people who adore him.

Ellie, an Angelic Beauty who also happens to be a princess of another Kingdom, is head over heels for him.

This is something he always dreamed of but never had because he considered himself to be a loser.

Trust me we all have felt like this.

A nerd who always surrounded himself with books and would always be in deep thought about science and magic now finds he has those powers he always fantasized about and read about in Japanese Mangas.

A Loser who always felt he was ignored find himself to be the centre of attention.

How will he cope with this drastic change in his life?

How will he use the magical power that he has acquired to be the protector of his realm?

How will he fight against the the evil forces who have been plotting for years to rule over this world?

In short it's a classic GOOD vs. EVIL tussle with a touch of magic,romance, erotica,action,adventure and fantasy.

If you want to read something with all those elements and if you want characters that you want to relate to, look no further than HAREM KING, conceptualized and written by my dear friend August D Heart.

Preface

If this isn't your first time reading a novel, then you are probably familiar with the words 'cliche or 'trope'. If you aren't familiar with it, it's a phrase or opinion that is overused or a figurative or metaphorical use of a word or expression. Novels, movies or animations; anime use them a lot and if you are someone like me who are fan of novels, movies or anime at some point, they become so repetitive you start to get bored of them, and everything starts to get predictable and spoil everything. I hated that, I thought I could write better stories than these. Thus, my one-year journey started and fortunately, I found a friend from the beginning to support and encourage me to keep going and complete my first novel. During my writing period, there was no shortage of ideas and content because of already available great stories from other authors whom I can't even give enough credit for. This novel is full of parodies and references from the original works of respective authors. I think along the journey the story didn't go the way I intended in the beginning, I just went with the flow not to force the story back on track since it would just ruin the story. Despite this, I think it turned out great for my first novel. I sincerely, thank you for purchasing and reading my first work. Hope you enjoy it,

Acknowledgements

I would like to express my sincere gratitude to the brilliant minds who have inspired me throughout my writing journey. The imaginative worlds created by Akira Toriyama, the captivating storytelling of Stan Lee and Steve Ditko, developer and creator of the game Genshin impact and the intricate character development of Masashi Kishimoto have left an indelible mark on my work. Their masterpieces have ignited my passion for storytelling and pushed me to strive for excellence. I am eternally grateful for their contributions to the world of literature and entertainment. Also I would like to express my heartfelt gratitude toward Notionpress in helping me publishing my novel costfree. Finally, I would like to thank Dinesh Rijal one of my closest friend who read and review my manuscript.

Prologue

In the heart of the Eastern Continent, a realm shrouded in ancient magic lies the magnificent Hellberg Kingdom. A place where dreams intertwine with destiny, and where the extraordinary is commonplace.

Our tale begins with Arthur Phoenix, a young prince destined for greatness. A prodigy in sorcery, he possesses a power that could reshape the very fabric of the world. Yet, beneath his regal facade, a troubled soul yearns for connection and understanding. Haunted by a tragic past, Arthur carries the weight of a secret that could shatter the kingdom's delicate balance.

As he embarks on a perilous journey, he will delve into the mysteries of his origins, confront formidable foes who seek to exploit his power and forge unbreakable bonds with a diverse cast of characters, each with their own unique strengths and vulnerabilities. In a world teeming with intrigue, love, and betrayal, he must navigate the treacherous path to his destiny, all while striving to protect those he holds dear.

CHAPTER ONE

BEGINNING AFTER THE END.

"...ness! ...majesty! Please wake up, Your Majesty!" a soft but persistent voice urged.

The young royal, lost in the realm of dreams, mumbled in response, "Hmm... 5 more minutes, Mom, let me kiss my cr... Zzz."

A sigh of exasperation followed. "Sigh! Your majesty, wake up, your breakfast is ready. You will be late for the coronation later."

But the prince's slumber remained unbroken, his snores continuing in a steady rhythm. "Zzz... Zzz... Zzz."

Frustration was evident, and the voice spoke again, "What happened? He isn't up yet?"

A servant, ever dutiful, replied, "Uh, young miss! No, unfortunately not. I have been trying to wake him up for hours, but his majesty doesn't seem to wake up."

Determined, the young lady took charge, her tone firm, "Let me try,... WAKE UP, YOU MORON! HOW LONG ARE YOU PLANNING TO LIE THERE LIKE A ROTTING CORPSE? HUH??"

The room was suddenly silent, broken only by a groggy voice, "....."

"AHHH! Who the heck kicked me...?!"

"WHO ELSE, YOU PIECE OF SHIT! YOUR NIGHTMARE!"

" Eiii... ll...ie?"

"Eille, my ass! Hurry up get ready, and come to the dining hall for breakfast. It's getting late."

"YES! MAM!"

In the realm of the Eastern continent's Hellberg Kingdom, Arthur Phoenix, at the tender age of 17, held a dual role - that of Throne Warmer, the unofficial title for the heir, and the Kingdom's Sorcerer. Today's forceful morning awakening came courtesy of his childhood friend and fiancée, a young woman of the same age whose outward demeanour belied her youth. With her silken white hair, deep blue eyes, and well-defined curves, she exuded a mature aura that often caught Arthur off guard. This, however, was not her only role; her name was not only attached to him through affection but also through the duties of a trusted personal aide named Maria, responsible for Arthur's every need and affair.

But Arthur's regal life was a far cry from his origins, a fact that required a journey back in time.

On February 22, 2022, he was known by a different name - August D. Heart. A college student engrossed in the pursuit of a bachelor's degree in science, his life was a cascade of misfortunes. Born under an unlucky star, nothing ever seemed to fall in place. His efforts yielded little, familial conflicts persisted, and the weight of solitude, betrayal, and a litany of other woes bore down on him. He reached out for support, only to be met with rejection. The burden of grief grew, threatening his sanity. There he stood on the precipice of existence, a single event away from toppling over the edge. But somehow, he clung to life, holding on by a thread.

Six months later, on August 3, 2022, that eventuality struck. The event he had dreaded materialized as another cherished relationship unravelled. No, it wasn't a demise, but the severing of a deep bond. A quarrel had driven a wedge between them. To August, it felt like a breakup, for the person he lost was not just a friend, but someone he deeply cherished. This was no ordinary friendship; it was a connection that defied rejection, a lifeline amidst a sea of solitude. And yet, his pride and jealousy had undermined it. His imperfections fueled this loss, a testament to his unwavering refusal to yield. This was his essence, shaped by an indomitable spirit he couldn't escape.

The cloud of loneliness and despair, along with an array of negative emotions, once in retreat, now surged back with tempestuous force. As they engulfed him, it was evident that these stormy feelings were beyond fleeting. By the time they struck, any hope of reversing their course had been swept away, leaving him in a whirlwind of emotions. Amidst this tempest, a mental breakdown ensued, rendering sleep a distant memory. His countenance bore the telltale signs of exhaustion - dark circles beneath his eyes, unruly hair, and clothing left untouched. Despite this, he trudged to college the next day, a reflection of the tumult within.

Then came that fateful day...

August 4, 2022

The blaring horns echoed in the air: "HONK! HONK!"

...

"HONK! HONK!"

...!

And then, a deafening crash shattered the cacophony.

The events of that day remain a mystery, even to the protagonist himself. Driven by some unseen force, he stepped heedlessly in front of an oncoming truck, heedless of the impending danger. His mind was a blank canvas, uncaring of the world or its inhabitants. It's often said that one's life flashes before their eyes when confronted by mortality, but in this case, there was nothing worth revisiting. With closed eyes and a faint smile, he welcomed the inevitable.

In the present time, as his eyes fluttered open, he found himself in the form of a six-year-old boy. It was a perplexing twist of fate, a reincarnation scenario that many light novel and anime enthusiasts might relish, including himself.

Don't delve too deeply into the mindset of our narrator and protagonist - they both share a penchant for anime and light novels and converse in the language of the otaku.

The question of why he hadn't been accused of abducting the kingdom's king and assuming his identity was a valid one. Yet, the answer lay in his memories. Not only did he retain recollections from his former life, but he also had access to the real Arthur's memories. The "how" of this phenomenon was as elusive to him as it was to those pondering the tale - a gap that science could not fill, save for theories of parallel world traversal or dimensional shifts.

With the confusion of his newfound circumstances aside, he delved into the heart of the matter: his journey to get married to as many beautiful women as possible and become the legendary Harem King. Yet, he paused, remarking, "Ah! Man, that hit the spot."

An exasperated sigh followed her proclamation. "Sigh! At least behave with some regality when you're awake. Jeez!"

With a nonchalant attitude, he retorted, "Yeah, yeah, whatever. What do you even know about being a king? Not that I have a clue either, keke!"

"Huh?! How dare you insinuate such a thing? I'll have you know, I was the daughter of-..."

"Yeah, yeah, we're all well-versed in your story. Daughter of the Emperor of the Eastern Empire, skilled in governance, the empire's eventual fall due to Western conflict and internal strife, your father's noble sacrifice for your sake, your escape, your ambush, and so on. We've heard it all countless times..."

"WHAT DID YOU JUST SAY?!"

"Simply put, we've all heard your tale numerous times – the rise, fall, and flight to safety. Not to mention how I found you when I was secretly honing my magical skills."

"Nevertheless, it's inexcusable to trivialize my past."

"I wasn't trivializing it. The saga has been repeated so often that the entire castle knows it by heart. We understand your hardships. So, please, not today. This is a momentous day, after all. You wouldn't want to cast a pall over it, would you?"

"Hmph! I'm done eating. I'm leaving first." With saddened and teary eyes Ellie leaves showing a hint of anger.

"Wait a moment, Ellie. Allow me to finish." Arthur followed after her regretting what he had done feeling guilty after seeing tears in her eyes.

"Ugh! What more do you want to say? I'm not interested in listening."

The silent corridor echoes with a stepping sound from Ellie as if they were rebelling against Arthur coming close to her.

As Arthur hurries to catch up with Ellie Arthur instructs Maria to distribute the leftover food among the servants and guards in the castle.

Maria objects but Arthur still insists without letting her finish and disappears round the corner as his voice fades into the silence in the hallways. With no choice, Maria agrees and follows what she's told.

The scene shifts to the hallway where Arthur finally catches up to Ellie and is seen trying to apologize.

"Ellie, wait! Please, listen. I apologize. I might have crossed a line this time. Can you find it in your heart to forgive me, just this once?"

"Listen to what? Are you already tired of me? No, I won't forgive you." Ellie turns her head in the opposite direction swelling her cheeks as if to show she is still angry and unhappy about it and thinks to herself

"Perhaps it's time to tease him a bit more. After all, he's always making fun of me. This is my chance for payback. Though he's genuinely sorry and has overstepped, it's not often I get such an opportunity. Let's have some fun with him."

"Forgive me, just this once. Pretty please. It doesn't quite befit a king to plead before someone. How about this: I'll grant one wish of yours, though nothing as outrageous as bringing the dead back to life. Will that earn your forgiveness?" Desperation and eager for forgiveness Arthur joins his hands and begs Ellie pleading to forgive him.

Unfazed by Arthur's pleading Ellie keeps her playfulness to torture Arthur further "*Ho! That's a tempting offer. Look at how cute he looks when he's slightly flustered.* Alright, I'll forgive you, but not immediately. I'll let you know when it's time. For now, we need to focus on the matter at hand."

The scene shifted to a bustling square where a massive crowd had gathered, stretching as far as the eye could see. A floating magical stone was present, recording and projecting the events onto the square. It served as a form of camera, powered by magic. In this world, science was less advanced, but magic compensated for its limitations. With an abundance of mana in this realm, magic was the preferred route over scientific advancements, echoing the themes of the isekai novels he had once avidly read.

As the sight before Arthur overwhelms him A thought comes across his mind. *"Damn! Do I have to give a speech? If that's the case, I'm utterly doomed. I didn't even prepare a speech, let alone practice one. I don't know how kings are supposed to address their people in this world. Just a decade ago, I was a mere college student. And now, I've been thrust into kingship. Before that, I was just a prince. Before the previous body's father, the former king, was murdered by an unknown assailant, the former owner of this body hadn't even witnessed his own father's coronation. The king's assassin remains at large, and the former owner was a mere child when all this unfolded. This is a predicament. I'll just wave my hand around, like how Queen Elizabeth used to do on Earth."*

As turning toward Arthur witnessing him completely frozen in nervousness in front of the crowds Ellie decides to take the helm in her hand. "Citizens of Hellberg Kingdom!" Ellie's voice rang out.

"We stand a few days past the dark day when our beloved monarch was brutally taken from us by a wretched scoundrel. Although he managed to escape unharmed that night, rest assured, we are committed to finding that vile creature and ensuring he pays dearly for his deeds. In these times, your hearts may have been heavy with sorrow, despair, and fear for your future, the futures of your families, friends, and our beloved kingdom. Yet, do not be disheartened. For a new dawn has arrived, bearing hope and illumination for our path forward, as ordained by the twelve council of ministers. Our second prince, Arthur Phoenix, stands as the embodiment of that hope and the guiding light for our kingdom's future. I understand you may be curious about the fate of the first prince. Allow me to clarify that he is currently absent from the kingdom due to pressing matters, out of contact for a while. We have made numerous attempts to establish communication but to no avail. However, we can confirm his survival through reports received, though not a single response. Due to the urgency of the situation, we were compelled to secure our kingdom's future, lest any adversaries capitalize on our vulnerability. Hence, the second prince has assumed the mantle of heir to the throne. And now, I yield the floor to our new sovereign, that he may offer words of encouragement and blessings upon our people."

With the closing of Ellie's speech, murmurs and chatter sound followed from the crowd.

Taking advantage of the moment Ellie insists Arthur speak his mind to the crowd "Hey, go ahead and say something. They're waiting," Ellie whispered.

"What? But I hadn't prepared anything. I wasn't aware I'd have to make a speech. What am I supposed to do?" Arthur replied, growing anxious.

Watching Arthur's Anxious and troubled expression Ellie threw some words of encouragement and advice for Arthur."You don't need to deliver a full-fledged speech. Just offer a few words of encouragement and praise. That should suffice."

Sigh "Fine, fine. Whatever." With No Choice, Arthur gives up and accepts it.

How did I get myself into this? What a headache...

"My esteemed citizens, I trust you are all in good health. If not, rest assured that you need not bear the burdens of this kingdom or your future alone. I solemnly pledge to safeguard my people and this realm with my very life.", Arthur muttered under his breath, *"Man, I can't believe I'm saying this. It's so cringeworthy. Someone, please rescue me.* I recognize it might be challenging to place your trust in a new leader. Nonetheless, I am committed to earning your confidence and proving myself worthy of this throne. You have toiled tirelessly for the sake of this land, your families, and your future. I salute your dedication even amidst these trying times. Going forward, I intend to alleviate some of your burdens, improve your quality of life, reinforce laws, and strive to lower crime rates as much as possible. I aim to ensure that none of you face a fate like mine. I implore your favour and wholehearted support as I embark on this journey."

Echoes of the applause and chants of high praises from the crowd spread throughout the squire.

"Long live the king! Long live the king!" The crowd erupted in cheers.

Witnessing the scene in disbelief Arthur thought to himself "Huh?! Did they like it? I had no idea what I was saying." Arthur decides to feign cluelessness and asks Ellie. "So, Ellie, what did you think?"

"It was alright, I suppose. But if you can't even manage that, what good are you?" Ellie remarked.

At the end of the speech, a sound followed attracting everyone's attention.

"Hmm, what is that sound?" Arthur inquired.

"It's the sound of a trumpet. It's played when a royal is either returning or arriving. I wonder who it could be." Ellie answered.

They moved forward, their gaze fixed on the screen.

As Arthur awaits in anticipation to see who has arrived at such a moment he thinks to himself "*If someone is arriving at this time, and going by the patterns of my previous life, this isn't going to end well. Every time I accomplish something, something goes awry. I sensed something was off when things were going smoothly. My gut feeling isn't sitting right.*"

The scene shifts to the castle gate where a group of shadows riding horses are entering.

Whisper, Murrmers and chatters fill among the crowds as they wait in anticipation.

"EVERYONE! Our Prince Francis has finally returned!" A voice rang out from the crowd.

"Prince Francis? He's back? Where?" Another voice chimed in.

"Look over there! Prince Francis has returned. Looks like we're saved. They said they couldn't get in touch with him. Were they lying?" A third voice spoke.

"Who knows? The truth will come out eventually. If their words were false, it could ignite a civil war. If that happens, we're done for," the second voice responded.

The crowd goes silent as the tip-tap sounds of horses come nearer and nearer.

A procession entered – ten cavalry knights, a hundred-foot soldiers, and the prince himself, resplendent in appearance. With his charming face, silky blond hair, and deep blue eyes that resembled the ocean, he exuded an air of confidence. His lean yet imposing figure was astride a white horse, its royal bearing commanding attention as they moved through the crowd towards the castle.

"Ah! Our prince is so captivating. A single glance and I feel like I might faint. If only I were a royal or even a noble, I could see him every day." A commoner girl swoons over the prince

The prince acknowledged the crowd with a wave and a slight smile.

"Did he just look at me and smile?!" The girl faints from over excitement and stimulation with the slight look and smile from the prince

"Hey, what's all the commotion about? Why is everyone gathered here?" Prince Francis inquired of a nearby soldier.

"Your Highness, it's a bit delicate... it seems we arrived a little too late. The twelve councils have already declared the second prince as the new monarch. And today was likely the coronation."

"Say what?!" The prince exclaimed, his voice inadvertently loud. "Calm down. Let's assess the situation first and then decide our course of action. What? They did what? Are you telling me they've declared that good-for-nothing, weakling, and timid brother as the heir to the throne?"

"I'm afraid that's accurate," the soldier confirmed.

Hearing the words from the soldier and witnessing the scene right before his eyes, Francis had no choice but to accept it but he wasn't going to let it down so easily. *"Damn it all! Damn it, damn it, damn it! This is unbelievable! After all the trouble and plotting I've done to secure my right to the throne, he's reaping the rewards. I won't stand for this. Little brother, enjoy your time while it lasts, for big bro has a surprise in store for you. Kekekeke!*

"Sigh! First, let's head to the castle and assess the situation. We should also congratulate my younger brother on his grand achievement," Prince Francis declared.

"Understood."

At that moment, He remained oblivious to the impending future, its ominous clouds casting a shadow over the kingdom—the beginning of the end, and the beginning after the end. Far above, someone from the infinity watched without intervention, betraying the hopes and beliefs of the people. When someone who should remain impartial shows favouritism, the sacred balance is disrupted, leading the world down an irrevocable path. He was the sole person who could halt this course, and at some point, He found the answer He sought.

Name: Arthur Phoenix

Age: 17 years old

Weight: 70kg

Height: 5'9"

Constellation: Leo

Personality: Righteous, strong-willed, persistent, courageous.

Likes: Anime, Novels, comics, games, Science and magic.

Dislikes: Hypocrites, betrayers, weak-natured people, kids.

Dreams: Nobel prize (past life), To be a king and have his own Harem (current).

Relationship: Engaged with Ellie.

Skills: Research, Magic Engineering, Martial Arts

Jobs: 3-star Mage, 2nd-star Magic Swordsman

Special Trait: Reincarnated.

CHAPTER TWO

BEGINNING OF THE END.

After reaching the castle, Francis went straight to the throne room, where Arthur and everybody else were discussing their matters. Francis had a calm and composite face as well as elegant movements without any slightest hints of frustration, anger and raging fury inside him. Francis had mastered the art of unwavering despite any situation he faced from a very young age. Because Francis believed that showing any kind of emotion outside is the same as revealing your weakness to your enemy.

Francis arrived at the door of the throne room guarded by two royal guards. They greeted the first prince and opened the door. Francis was welcomed by the fancily decorated room full of people of royalties and nobles waiting for his return.

"I bow and greet the majesty." Francis calmly greets Arthur not letting to show the hint of his inner thoughts. *"Fuck Fuck Fuck! How dare you make me kneel in front of you. You are just a weakling who knows nothing about the outside world, who only immerses himself in books and plays around the whole day without care in the world."*

Surprised but not letting to show for it in front of the crowd Arthur welcomes Francis cheerfully" Ah! Welcome! Welcome brother. It's finally good to see you." Arthur pauses in panic as Francis bows before him and soon after he continues "*From previous Arthur's memory, I had only supposedly seen him in his teenage and he had a nasty personality. I need to be careful with details if I am gonna play this right.* No, no. What are you doing brother, you don't have to be so formal."

Arthur quickly gets up from his seat and insists on him to stand up and hugs him thinking to himself. *"Sigh! Why do I have to do this cringy stuff, being a king sometimes is such a drag. Technically, I don't even know him nor do I have any brotherly love toward him. He is a total stranger to me. Is this some kind of BL novel or something?"*

"Brother, I missed you so much. I am glad you finally returned home."Arthur speaks keeping his poker face.

Despite feeling some things off and odd about Arthur, Francis humours Arthur's poker face with his and congratulates Arthur. "I missed you too little bro. It's finally good to be home. And congratulations on taking our father's position. It's a huge responsibility so I hope you will see it to the end and work hard for the sake of the kingdom."

"There's something off about him. The more I look at him, the more it pisses me off. Goddess, should I kill him now? I can't feel but something wrong here." Francis asks the goddess who had shown favour to him quietly observing from the shadows.

Goddes replies in refute to Francis's appeal. "There is no need for that now. I have lost half my power breaking the rules and making a contract with you. If we do anything that will attract the attention of other gods before I regain my power then we will be in big trouble. I can neither protect you nor myself. So wait for me to regain my power before you do anything stupid. *YAWN* I am getting sleepy so see ya later."

Arthur replies confidently shifting toward feeling guilty placing his hand on his chest. "Indeed, dear brother. I am determined to not let you or the kingdom's citizens down. I'll spare no effort in meeting everyone's expectations. Also, I deeply regret being the cause of your rights being taken away. I initially declined, but circumstances forced my hand. I had little choice."

Francis laughed it off and replied, "No worries, little brother.The timing was crucial, and I understand why it had to be done. You acted appropriately." Rest of his sentence, Francis continued in his mind. "*But It will eventually be mine again.* "

Feeling he is at his limit Arthur changes the subject and drives the conversation toward the end. "If that's your stance, big brother, then I shall respect it. You must be fatigued from your long journey. I suggest you rest for the remainder of today. We can convene to discuss matters tomorrow."

Just as Arthur mentioned the fatigue from the journey that he had forgotten rushes over his body again. Thinking this was a good opportunity Francis agrees with Arthur and takes his leave. "If my younger brother insists, I have no choice. Until tomorrow, then."

As Francis left All kinds of thoughts started to plague Arthurs's mind. "*This is his disposition, then. Quite a charismatic figure. I can't help but envy him. Why can't I have a fraction of his charm? In both my lives, I've received nothing of the sort. Based on memories, the former king had two wives; one was of common birth but passed away giving birth to Francis. He seems to have been graced by the goddess Freya, representing beauty and war, from the moment of his birth. His looks and personality have earned him the people's adoration. I hate such types of people so much.*"

Francis noticed Ellie standing in a corner and approached her. "*Hmm?! Why does she seem familiar?* Pardon me, young lady, but I don't believe I've seen you here before. I am Francis Pheonix, the first prince of the Hellberg Kingdom. Would you kindly introduce yourself?"

Flustered from the sudden approach from the first prince Ellie replies in a soft voice "Umm...me? I am Arthur's fiancée, Ellie Charlotte." On a closer look, Ellie sees a very familiar face that she has seen once before, she greets Francis elegantly thinking to herself "*Oh god, why is he here? I hope he doesn't recognize me. If he does, I'm as good as dead. And Arthur's safety would be jeopardized because of me. I must tell Arthur the truth about this guy.*"

"Hmm, Have we crossed paths before? Your face holds a sense of familiarity." Francis asks in curiosity bringing his face closer to Ellie.

By the second Ellie starts to lose composer but she still manages to hold her ground."*EEKK! He's getting close to exposing me. I need to manage this situation. Stay calm and respond before he grows more suspicious.* I don't think so, Your Highness. You might be confusing me with someone else."

Francis not wanting to attract too much attention backs down. "Yes, I am exhausted, so that is plausible. I apologize, Excuse me for now. *But This is odd, though. There's no way I could mistake her for another person. I wouldn't forget someone I've met before. She's hiding something, and I must uncover the truth. *TSK!* Issues just keep piling up.*"

Leaving the throne room after the encounter with Ellie, Francis was filled with doubt and suspicion. Fatigued from the journey, he made his way directly to his quarters. Before entering, he summoned his most trusted butler, Alfred, a former top-star mercenary with a robust build. He entrusted Alfred with the task of preventing any disturbances or unauthorized entry into his quarters.

Francis flops on his bed thinking about all the things that happened in the single day he arrived. "*Phew! What a day. Finally, I can relax in my little sanctuary. Alright, before I collapse from all these exhausting affairs, I should tackle them one by one, then take a nap.*

"So, what's our next move?" the goddess communicated through telepathy.

Francis replies in frustration, "Oh, why must you interject now? Never mind. I don't have the energy to argue with you right now. Our priority is identifying that mysterious individual. We'll address Arthur later. He poses little immediate threat. Although his magical prowess is considerable, my power surpasses his, especially after our pact. Both my swordsmanship and martial skills have seen substantial enhancement through rigorous training."

Goddess replies in a smug but uncertain tone in her voice, "Indeed, you've perceived that aspect. But you've overlooked the crux of the matter. The soul within his body is not the same as before. Upon closer inspection, it appears to originate from another world. This demands caution. We're uncertain of his capabilities or concealed motives. Another god may be at play here. Yet, regardless of the agent, complacency is not an option. Underestimating the enemy is perilous."

Feeling already tired Francis tries to end the conversation as soon as possible. "Yes, yes, I've heard your counsel. Now, leave me alone and let me handle my responsibilities."

Feeling as if being ignored goddess replies in a higher angrier tone. "Goodness, could you perhaps exhibit a smidgeon of politeness, you wretched rascal? Your appearance is the only semblance of value you contribute, and even that originates from me. In any case, remain vigilant for both our well-being."

Goddess's nagging frustrates Francis more, and with no choice but to listen to her, Francis makes up his mind to finish his final task for the day. "Ugh! She's such a headache. Anyway, where were we? Ah, right. About that individual."

Francis moved to the nearest shelf and retrieved a slightly bluish magical orb. He infused a trace of magic into it, causing it to emit a soft glow. He then began to call out a name. "Black, are you available?"

"Yes, my lord. How can I be of assistance?" responded a voice.

"Commence an investigation on Arthur's fiancée, Ellie Charlotte. Keep her and Arthur under vigilant observation. Report their activities consistently." Francis commanded voice echoed through the orb as black listened

In absolute loyalty, Black responded, "Of course, my lord."

The light and voice from the orb disappear the conversation ends but Francis's mind is still not free from other thoughts. "*That settles one matter. I'll address Arthur later. What remains is dealing with the 12 councils. Those elderly individuals have gained audacity. I must eliminate those clinging to power even as they teeter on the edge of the grave. It's time for some changes.*"

Francis once more infused the orb with magic, causing it to illuminate. "Red, I require your service."

"Yes, my lord. How may I assist you?" A low-pitched voice resounded from the orb.

As before Francis commands "I want you to systematically eliminate each member of the 12 councils, ensuring no mistakes or mishaps. Can you fulfil this task?"

"It's possible, but meticulous planning and preparations will be necessary, not to mention time." The high-pitched voice replies in an ambiguous tone

Francis, not caring about anything but the result permits us to take any necessary steps to get the result."I'm indifferent to the specifics. You have my full authorization. Employ any means necessary to eliminate them."

"Understood." The high-pitched voice responded quickly and disconnected.

"Sigh! That settles matters. I can finally indulge in a lengthy rest. Yawn! It's certainly advantageous to have the 'Black Order' and 'The Crows' functioning as my eyes, ears, and instruments." Francis drifted into slumber as soon as he lay down. Unaware of the truth regarding his younger brother, who he believed was no more, replaced by another.

The following day, in the early morning,

As usual, Arthur was engrossed in his magical experiments, drawing upon the scientific knowledge he possessed. He covertly honed his mana, developed new spells, and refined existing ones within his clandestine training chamber, a space known only to himself and Ellie.

Exhausted from the training Arthur flops to the ground and starts revising everything he has learned in his head, "*Alright, there are five fundamental elemental magics: Fire, Water, Earth, Wind, and Lightning, along with three attribute magics: Light or Holy, Shadow or Dark, and Null or Space. I've absorbed this information from the memories I've inherited. Yet, the challenge lies in creating new spells. My repeated attempts at crafting time-based attribute magic have met failure. For now, let's concentrate on enhancing the existing repertoire.*

"Arthur, I've been searching for you all morning. I have something important to discuss." A soft and rigid interrupts Arthur attracting his attention.

Sewaty from his training Arthur welcomes Ellie wiping away his sweats. "Hey, Ellie. What's up? Why were you looking for me?"

"Well... You see..." Ellie speaks hesitantly but before she finishes Arthur pulls her over excitedly. "Never mind that for now. I want to show you something."

"But it's really important!" Ellie mutters, frustrated. "He's absorbed in his magic experiments again. Well, what do you want to show me?"

"I'm about to unleash KAMEHAMEHA!" Arthur announces enthusiastically.

"Kame-hame-what now?" Ellie's confusion deepens.

"Just watch carefully and don't blink." Arthur excited to show Ellie takes a stance lowering his body.

Not knowing what Arthur is up to Ellie agrees anyway and plays along. "Alright..."

Not to make mistakes or miss any step Arthur resiites the plan in his head. *"Here's the plan: I'll cover my hands with a thin layer of earth and wind magic to shield them from the intense heat. Then, I'll ignite the fire with my fire magic and gradually expand it to the size of a ball. After that, I'll cautiously compress it using wind magic to prevent it from extinguishing. Finally, when it's compressed into a plasma state, I'll meticulously extract oxygen atoms while simultaneously supplying it with hydrogen atoms to sustain the fuel cycle. At this point, it becomes extremely hot and equally destructive. Here goes nothing. End of an impromptu physics lesson Ehehe."*

"KA-ME-HA-ME-HAAA!" Arthur unleashes the spell.

WHOOSH! A laser-like beam shoots out from Arthur's hands, colliding with a wall nearly 50 feet away and leaving a crater about 5 feet in diameter.

BANG! BOOOM!

That completely caught Ellie off-guard. Ellie couldn't believe what she just saw and the sight before her eyes. "WHAT THE

HELL, ARTHUR? What was that? I've never seen or heard of magic like that. Why is your fire blue, and why is it so incredibly destructive?"

"Well, it's something I recently devised—a fusion of let's just say laws of this world called physics and magic, emulating something every kid from the past dreamed of at some point in their life. For me, that dream has become a reality. I've wanted to try that for ages. Unfortunately, it consumes an enormous amount of magic power. I can only maintain it for a split second, and it's inefficient for combat due to its long charging time. In battle, every second is precious, making it more of a last-resort option."

Not Understanding a word Arthur said Ellie continued scolding Arthur. "That's just insane! Are you planning to wipe out an entire kingdom or what?"

Arthur hearing Ellie sounding so ridiculous couldn't help but let out a laugh and spoke, "Haha, no. It may seem flashy, but it drains a considerable portion of my magical reserves. Besides, it's not practical for fights. By the time it's ready to fire, I'd likely be defeated."

"Speaking of which, you look worn out and you're sweating a lot. Are you okay?" Ellie asks Arthur with a concerned expression.

"Yeah, I'm fine. Tota...ly f...i...n...e..." Arthur's voice trails off, and he collapses.

Thud! Arthur collapses on the ground before Ellie can get hold of him."Arthur, are you alright? You don't look well. Should I call for help?" Ellie panics.

Still hanging on but on the verge of losing consciousness, Arthur rest assured Ellie. "I'm fine, Ellie. Just a bit dizzy. Rest will fix it. I think I've run out of mana."

Hearing reassurance Ellie breathes a sigh of relief. "Okay, that's a relief. You can rest your head on my lap. I'll stay with you until you feel better."

Before Arthur reaches his limit and loses consciousness Arthur thanks Ellie. "Thanks, Ellie. You're kind t..o..d..a..y... ZZZ!"

"Yeah, because it might not be long before I'm not around anymore," Ellie speaks smiling stroking Arthur's hair softly with a bit of sadness in her eyes.

That day, he made a significant mistake by not heeding her concerns, and to this day, he regrets it. If only he had listened, he wouldn't have to carry that regret. He recognized her worry, yet he disregarded it, and she responded with a warm smile. If given another chance, he'd make a different choice. He had been so absorbed in the power of his knowledge and magic that he overlooked the importance of experience and practical skills. In this harsh world, knowledge alone couldn't guarantee success. Experience was crucial for handling various situations.

Late afternoon:

Arthur was engrossed in his office tasks when he heard a knock on the door. KNOCK! KNOCK!

Wondering who could it be Arthur asks, "Who is it?"

"It's your big brother, my dear little brother." A familiar annoying voice came from the door.

"Oh, yes, please come inside," Arthur replied as Francis entered the room. "But what brings you here today? Is everything alright?"

Francis replies nonchalantly with a smile on his face."Everything's fine. Does a big brother need a reason to visit his younger brother? I'm just here to see how you're adjusting to your new life. If there's anything I can help with, don't hesitate to ask."

"Sure." Arthur forces a smile and shows forced enthusiasm.

Before Arthur could catch a breath Francis strikes with a question. "By the way, I was wondering, how did you meet Ellie and where is she from?"

Arthur tries to avoid Francis after finally getting the chance."Oh, right, I completely forgot. I haven't properly introduced you two, have I? I should call her right away. Just wait here for a minute."

Noticing Arthur's Intention Francis Stops Arthur in his tracks. "Uh, no need. It's fine. She's probably busy. We've already met and introduced ourselves. I was just curious since she looks somewhat familiar to me."

"Is that so?" Arthur can't help but race his mind as he tries to figure out what is francis up to. "*Why is he asking about Ellie? Could he have a crush on her? No, no, that's not it. There's no way he would do that, right? And even if he did, I wouldn't let it happen.*"

Arthur reminisces as he tells the story of how he met Ellie. "Well, I met her when I was 6 years old in a small village in the countryside. She was injured and alone at that time, so I took her in. She mentioned being from the Eastern Empire and running away from attackers."

Sympathising to Arthur's words Francis responds in a regretful note "It's unfortunate what she went through. I heard the Eastern Empire was completely devastated, and the royal family didn't survive. It's a relief she managed to escape."

"Well, actually, this is confidential information, but not all of the royals were killed. She's the daughter of the emperor and the last remaining bloodline." Arthurs lowers his voice whispering as he speaks.

"What? Is that true?" Eyes Widened in surprise Francis Inquires if it's true. "*No wonder she looked familiar. She resembles her father a lot. The one who escaped came right to the lion's den, huh? This just got even more interesting.*"

"Yeah, so I hope you'll keep this a secret, big brother." Arthur continues in a lower voice whispering.

"Of course, I'll keep this secret to my grave." Francis thumps up grinning and promises to keep it a secret.

A knock on the door diverts their attention. KNOCK! KNOCK!

"Yes, please come in," Arthur responds.

"Hey, Arthur, do you have a moment?... Oh! Greetings, Prince Francis. I hope I'm not interrupting anything." Francis's presence took Ellie by surprise.

"No, we were just chatting. Alright, I'll leave you two alone. But don't get too carried away in there, okay?" Francis teases before leaving.

"BROTHER!" Arthur exclaims, his face turning red.

Ellie blushes in the corner, her index fingers nervously touching.

To break the awkwardness Arthur starts by apologizing to Ellie "I'm so sorry, Ellie. Please forgive my brother's behaviour. He can be quite insensitive at times. *What was that? Is he always like this? Or could he be teasing Ellie because he's interested in her? I can't quite figure him out.*"

"It's fine. But what you said, I wouldn't mind doing it with you," Ellie mumbles softly.

"Huh? Did you say something? *I thought I heard something, but let's just pretend I didn't hear it.*" Arthur responds, a slight blush creeping onto his face.

Feeling embarrassed to repeat it Ellie avoids the topic. "No, nothing at all. *I should change the topic.* Anyway, I was saying, are you free right now?"

"Hmm... I'm always free for you, my dear. What's on your mind?" Arthur smirks playfully, his thoughts betraying his teasing.

Ellie fidgeting and anxious musters up the courage to finally speak."Well, you see... Since it's been a while since we've gone outside, I thought maybe we could go undercover and see how the people are doing."

"Oh, I see. So you're suggesting we go on a little outing today?" Arthur's smirk persists.

"I wasn't asking you out on a date or anything like that, okay?" Ellie blushes and pouts, her emotions a mix of embarrassment and frustration.

"Haha, you're quite the adorable tsundere, aren't you? You're like an angry little hamster when you pout. Alright, I'll go out with you, but I have one condition," Arthur smirks inwardly, planning to push Ellie's boundaries a bit.

"One condition? What is it?" Ellie's curiosity grows as she meets Arthur's eyes.

"You'll have to give me a kiss right here," Arthur points to his lips with a playful gleam in his eyes.

Her heart races and her blood flow rises her ear starts to turn red, Embarrassed Ellie retaliates, "Eh?! But it's not that I don't want to or that I can't do it. It's just that... even though we're engaged, we haven't even held hands yet. This is too much for me right now."

Although Ellie says that her mind thinks completely differently. *"What are you saying, you idiot? This is a chance to deepen your relationship with him. It might be the only chance you get. Who knows what that so-called Prince Francis, the wolf in sheep's clothing, could be plotting right now?"*

"Well, alright. If you can't do it, I'll get back to my work," Arthur teases, smirking.

"No, wait. I'll do it, but you have to close your eyes." Feeling humiliated, Ellie avoided eye contact to hide her embarrassment

"Alright, I'll close my eyes." Arthur plays along with Ellies whimsical wishes.

"No, first promise me you won't peek." Not trusting Arthur one bit Ellie covers Arthur's eyes shut.

Though Arthur agrees and plays along with her he keeps picking on her to make fun of her."Fine, I promise I won't peek. Are you satisfied now? But I didn't promise I'd forget it, hehe..."

"Umm." Ellie fidgets and blushes, her voice barely audible. "Here I go."

Drawing closer to him, Ellie hesitates for a moment before gently pressing her lips against his. They both feel their hearts racing, their breaths mingling in the air. Arthur supports his forehead against hers, his eyes closed as he savours the moment. Slowly, he inches closer, his eyes gradually opening to capture every second of the fleeting moment. When he feels he's fully experienced the sensation, he closes the gap between them and they share their first kiss.

"Now, can we go?" Ellie asks, tugging at Arthur's arm.

"Yes, yes, I understand. So stop pulling. Sigh, what a hassle." Arthur and Ellie discreetly leave the castle, disguised as commoners, and make their way into the city.

"Arthur, where are we headed?" Ellie's eyes shine with excitement.

Ellie's words make Arthur confused so he asked, "Huh? Why are you asking me? I thought you had something in mind since you suggested going out."

"Hehe, actually I don't. Sorry about that." Ellie feigns innocence.

Annoyed by Ellie's answer with no choice left Arthur decides to take the lead. "Ugh, what a drag... So where do you want to go then? Do you have any place in mind?"

"Hmm, oh, I know! Let's start by going to Vendor Street. I haven't had lunch yet, and I'd love to try some street food." A clear excitement and joy cover her beautiful face with sparkling eyes of anticipation waiting ahead.

As his stomach growls in hunger he remembers he also hadn't eaten anything as well. "Come to think of it, I haven't eaten either. Okay, let's head to the vendor street first."

As they walk through the crowded street, a person in a brown robe collides with Ellie. She suddenly stops in her tracks, her grip on Arthur's hand loosening. She looks down and notices a dagger protruding from her stomach. Panic floods her as she realizes she's been stabbed. Arthur senses Ellie's distress and turns around to see her falling to the ground. He quickly catches her and finds his hand covered in her blood. His shock is palpable as he stares at Ellie, who is fading in and out of consciousness. He urges her to stay with him, to keep her eyes open and remain awake. Taking immediate action, he begins administering first aid.

Arthur cleans the area around the dagger wound with water, carefully diverts the blood circulation to avoid excessive bleeding, and binds the wound with a torn piece of cloth from his shirt. Realizing that removing the dagger would worsen the situation, he decides to leave it in place until he can get Ellie to a physician.

A small crowd gathers around them, curious about what's happening. Arthur, unfamiliar with the area due to his limited outings from the castle, rushes around asking people for the address of a physician. Unfortunately, nobody speaks up until a girl who looks only a few years younger than his age, with dirt-covered and tattered clothes, with bare feet steps forward and offers assistance. She had violet-coloured hair and eyes with a serious expression on her face. At a glance, her constitution looked weak and malnourished which she needed help with yet she was the only one who stepped forward among any of them.

The comes to Arthur and speaks in a weak and ragged voice "I know where the physician's place is, sir. I can show you the way if you'd like."

"Of course, please lead the way." Having no choice at his disposal Arthur decides to trust the girl and follow her

With Ellie in his arms, Arthur follows the girl's lead. Ellie has lost consciousness by now, but Arthur keeps trying to rouse her, his words a mix of desperation and concern. As they reach the physician's clinic, Arthur rushes inside and urgently calls for the physician. The physician immediately guides Arthur to place Ellie on a stretcher and helps carry her to the operation room. Arthur is struck by the efficiency of the emergency response, even in this world that lags behind his previous life in scientific advancement.

With Ellie in the hands of medical professionals, Arthur finally lets out a sigh of relief. Exhaustion from his earlier sprint catches up with him, and he collapses onto the ground, his back against the wall.

As Arthur sits there, his emotions overwhelming him, the girl who had guided him to the physician's place joins him. She sits beside him, offering silent comfort and understanding. Arthur is lost in his thoughts, drowning in the turmoil within his mind.

"Why? Why me? Why is it always me? When will this bad luck leave me alone? Was it not enough that it ruined my past life? Now it's affecting this one too. What did I do to deserve this? How much more suffering do I have to endure? Everyone around me suffers because of me. When will it all end? I thought my past life's ordeal was over, but it seems it's not. Because of me, Ellie got hurt today, and it will be someone else tomorrow. Is it even right for me to be with someone? Maybe I should just isolate myself and live alone. But before that, I will find and eliminate the person who did this to her. "

In Arthur's heart, a seed of hatred begins to grow, threatening to consume him in its flames.

Two hours later...

The physician finally emerged from the operating room, delivering the reassuring news that Ellie was going to be alright, albeit needing a few days of rest. Upon hearing this, Arthur wasted no time and hurried to Ellie's side. His eyes held a mixture of pain and relief, and he struggled to find the right words to say to her. But Ellie, breaking the silence, spoke first.

"Hey, why the gloomy face? I'm not dead, you know. It's just a minor scratch, nothing to get worked up about. A few days of rest, or we could ask a holy priest for a healing spell. Although I doubt they'd be interested in something so small." Despite her condition, Ellie tries to cheer up Arthur putting the tough act to not worry him further than he already has been.

"No, if it wasn't for me, you wouldn't have been in this situation. It's all my fault. I'm truly sorry, Ellie. I couldn't protect you, and I'm beginning to question whether I'm even fit to be a king, let alone your fiancé. Maybe I'm just not cut out for this—" Ellie intercepts Arthur's pessimistic train of thought with a flick on his forehead.

Ellie with a stern and displeased expression starts lecturing Arthur. "What on earth are you talking about? Who said any of this was your fault? I'm the one who suggested we go out. And who said you didn't protect me? You got me here, and I'm alive, right? That's all that matters. You're more than capable as my fiancé and as the king of this realm. So don't even entertain the idea that you're not enough."

Arthur's self-blame seemed to resonate deeply with Ellie, and she wanted to set his worries straight. Ellie continued. "However, if you're truly troubled, let me tell you this: accidents happen, and sometimes they're inevitable. Don't let this weigh on you. Also, please be careful not to take reckless actions that might tarnish your image in the eyes of the people. You're admired and respected by them, so you must tread carefully. That's all I can say, because knowing you, there's no stopping you from pursuing justice, right?"

Name: Francis Phoenix
Age: 26
Weight: 80 kg
Height: 6'0"
Constellation: Aquarius
Personality: Charming, ambitious, strategic, charismatic, manipulative, and complex.
Likes: Power, art, politics, strategy, elegance.
Dislikes: Incompetence, betrayal, vulnerability, trivial matters.
Dreams: Absolute rule, kingdom reform.
Relationship: Complex with Arthur, intrigued by Ellie.
Skills: Diplomacy, strategy, swordsmanship, espionage.
Jobs: Heir, political affairs, connections with nobles.
Special Trait: Photographic memory.

CHAPTER THREE

Searching Information

The Eastern Continent, one of the three powerhouse continents in this vast world, is a region defined by longstanding political divides and formidable factions. Two primary power blocs dominate this land: the Eastern Empire, a coalition of regions ruled under the Emperor's authority, and the Western Independent Parties, a loose alliance of five distinct kingdoms. These include Elfheim, the mystical home of the Elves; Nelfheim, inhabited by stout and skilled Dwarves; Helheim, the dark domain of Demons; Midgard, known as the human kingdom of Hellberg in honour of its heroic founder; and Asgard, a kingdom revered as a bastion of holiness.

Once, the Empire's influence maintained a relatively stable balance of power across these lands. However, internal strife, conflicts among the noble houses, and civil wars eventually drove the Empire to the brink of collapse. As its influence waned, regions formerly under imperial control became ripe for conquest, drawing the attention of neighbouring factions. Refugees fleeing the chaotic lands only worsened the situation, becoming pawns in the territorial ambitions of opportunistic dukes. This turmoil has begun spilling over into Hellberg, where tensions between supporters of the new king and the return of the 1st prince threaten to plunge the kingdom into civil war—a conflict with Arthur and Ellie precariously trapped in the middle.

Helheim Kingdom

Within the shadowy halls of Helheim's citadel, Lord Bohr receives intelligence about the shifting power dynamics in Hellberg.

"Alfred, what's the situation in Hellberg?" Lord Bohr inquires, his voice heavy with anticipation. "I've heard the 1st prince has returned, and his younger brother has claimed the throne. Is this true?"

"Lord Bohr, yes, that's correct," Alfred responds with a respectful bow. "The 12 councils in Hellberg decided to appoint the 2nd prince as their ruler before the 1st prince's return. Now, Hellberg is simmering with tension as both factions prepare for an inevitable clash. It's only a matter of time before open conflict breaks out."

Lord Bohr leans back, considering his options carefully. "Hmm... This seems like an opportune time to make our move," he muses aloud, "but that damn Francis is there. It would be suicide to act while he's present; the man is utterly unpredictable. We'll have to wait patiently or craft an opportunity. Perhaps we can manipulate Arthur into dealing with Francis on our behalf. Very well," he declares decisively. "Let's proceed with that plan. Deploy spies to gather intelligence and maintain a close watch on the developments in Hellberg. If I know Francis's character, he'll undoubtedly go after Arthur, and it's high time Arthur begins his intelligence operations."

Alfred nods in understanding. "Yes, my lord. Our scouts are prepared and awaiting further orders."

The tension in the kingdom of Hellberg is almost palpable, with factions manoeuvring in anticipation of conflict. Meanwhile, In a quieter corner of Hellberg, Ellie's eyes opened groggily, greeted by Arthur's familiar presence.

"Ellie, how are you feeling?" Arthur asked a gentle concern in his voice.

"Better than yesterday, I suppose," she replied with a faint smile.

Arthur handed her a small vial. "Here, it's time for your medicine."

Ellie hesitated, looking at him with suspicion. "Thank you... but why are you here, Arthur? Don't you have other responsibilities?

Where's Maria?"

Arthur hesitated before responding. "I asked Maria to let me bring your medicine. I... wanted to speak to you in private."

"And what is it that you want to discuss?" Ellie asked, her curiosity piqued.

Arthur sighed, his face conflicted. "I wanted to apologize again for not protecting you better. And I need to leave on a pressing matter. I'll be away for a few days, and I was hoping you could oversee things while I'm gone. I know it's selfish after what happened, but... there's no one I trust more than you."

Ellie's brow furrowed, but she nodded with a sigh. "You're always so hard on yourself. Fine, I'll cover for you—but only for three days, understood?"

Arthur's face softened with gratitude. "Thank you, Ellie. I promise that when all this is over, I'll marry you."

Ellie's cheeks flushed, and she sputtered, "Eek! Don't say things like that out of the blue! You will jinx it. You better come back in one piece, or I'll find a way to bring you back just to kill you myself."

In the dimly lit Crow Guild, Francis convened with his men and outlined the final stages of his sinister plan.

"Red, is the assassination plan ready to commence?" Francis asked.

"Yes, my lord. We'll strike tonight, right after the final bell. The team is briefed and ready."

"Good," Francis said coldly, his gaze sharp. "Remember, there is no room for error. I want those council members dead by dawn. Failure is not an option."

The men nodded, and as Francis left to solidify his influence, the scene shifted to yet another corner of Hellberg.

At the Cat's Tail Tavern, patrons watched as Francis made his way inside. Whispers swept through the room, with many wondering about the prince's sudden visit.

In the tavern's basement, Francis met with his undercover agents from the Black Order.

"Black, have you found anything about Arthur or Ellie in my absence?" Francis asked.

"My lord, we've observed that Arthur's behaviour has shifted dramatically. He's been attracting attention—especially from the 12 council members—with his recent actions and seems to have gained a stronger following."

Francis smirked. "Interesting. He did appear different when I saw him. Something in him has changed, though I don't know what."

As he concluded the meeting, Francis instructed his agents to continue monitoring Arthur closely, with orders to eliminate any informants who threatened to leak information.

In a soft candle-lit chamber, Arthur spoke to Maria as he prepared to depart.

"Oh, Maria, I thought you had already left for the evening," Arthur said, surprised to see her.

Maria curtsied and replied, "My place is always by your side, Your Grace."

Arthur smiled. "Take care of Ellie in my absence, will you? I may not return for some time, but her well-being is in your hands. And by the way, where's the girl I brought here last time?"

"She's resting in the adjacent room, Your Grace," Maria informed him.

Arthur approached the girl in the next room, the one who helped him not long ago. She looked up, surprised but grateful.

"Hey, how are you holding up?" Arthur asked gently. "I hope you haven't been too uncomfortable here. This situation must be strange and unsettling for you, huh? But I couldn't just leave you alone on the streets, could I?"

The girl's eyes welled up and in a trembling voice, she responded, "No, I'm fine. I'm so grateful for everything Your Grace has done for someone like me."

Arthur attempted to console her, "Woah, woah, don't cry. Did I say something wrong? Please, don't cry. Can you tell me what happened? Does anything hurt anywhere?"

"No...HICK! No HICK! No, it's just that I've never been this happy before in my entire life. I never thought I would ever get to enter such a big, grand, and important place. It's an honour to be here with you, Your Majesty," she tearfully expressed her gratitude.

Arthur, amused by her emotional response, assured her, "Huh? Is that all? No need to worry about small stuff. Now that you are here, you don't need to worry about anything while I am around. Pick yourself up from the ground, young lady. We have a job to do, and you are coming with me, got that?"

"Yes!" she replied enthusiastically.

Arthur continued, "Alright, I haven't asked your name, have I? So, what's your name?"

She introduced herself, "My name? It's Momo."

"Okay, Momo. I need your help. Can you help me?" Arthur inquired.

Momo responded with unwavering dedication, "Yes, of course. I will do anything you say, Your Majesty."

Arthur, cautioning her, added, "Oh?! Are you sure about that? You shouldn't go around saying such things, you know; people might take advantage of that."

Momo quickly clarified, "No-no, I am only saying this because it's you. You are giving me food, shelter, and clothing. I can't thank you enough. I am in your debt, so it's the last thing I could do to repay it."

Arthur appreciated her sentiment, saying, "Hmm. If it's like that, then it's okay, I guess. If that's the case, you can drop the formalities. You can just call me 'lord Arthur."

Momo hesitated but eventually agreed, "Yes, my lord."

Satisfied, Arthur asked calmly and politely, "Then if that's settled, Can you answer something for me?"

Momo tilts her head wondering but agrees anyway. "Okay."

Hearing a positive response from Momo, Arthur couldn't hold his excitement and In the heat of the moment grabbed Momo's solder and asked, "Since you were in the streets, you must have picked on a bunch of information. So by any chance Do you know where the information Guild is?"

Momo confirmed her understanding, "Yes."

Later, Arthur and Momo made their way through the bustling Liyue streets toward the information guild. He noticed Francis leaving the Cat's Tail Tavern as they passed, his expression one of calculation.

"Wait... wasn't that my brother?" Arthur muttered, watching Francis disappear into the distance. Arthur continued in his thoughts. " *Yes, it's him alright. No one else except royals is allowed to wear that crest. So the question is, what was he doing in the tavern and in the middle of the day? Why do I feel like something's wrong here? Should I follow him?* "

Momo tugged at his sleeve, breaking his thoughts."Lord, is there something wrong? Why did you stop all of a sudden?"

Arthur brushed off his suspicions, responding, "Oh, it's nothing. I just felt like I saw someone I knew. I must have been mistaken." Arthur continued his thoughts, "*No, it's not a good time right now. I have Momo with me. If something's wrong here, then I can't put her in danger, like I did with Ellie.*"

Understanding his hesitation, Momo encouraged, "Alright, we are just about there. We should go now."

Arthur agreed and strategized, "*Hmm, I will check this out when I am done with the information guild and alone. Maybe I can look up something at night. It's not a bad idea; let's go with that.*"

Eventually, they arrived at the information guild, a nondescript building hidden among the bustling stalls.

"This is it?" Arthur asked, puzzled by the building's humble appearance.

Momo nodded. "Yes, it may look unassuming, but this is the most trusted information guild currently in Hellberg only known to several people."

A loud hoarse voice interrupted with a greeting, "Oh, hello, dear customer. It's been a while since someone visited this place. So, what can I get you?"

As the middle-aged owner emerged from the pitch-black room holding a knife, Momo responded, "A crow hunt by the fox."

Arthur, utterly confused and surprised, muttered, "Say what?"

The owner gestured for them to follow, saying, "Right this way."

The situation unfolding in front of him made him even more confused and puzzled. *"Is it me, or did the mood suddenly change here? For now, let's just go with what she does. "*

Unsure about the situation, Arthur whispered to Momo, "Hey, Momo, are we in the right place? I'm sceptical about this place."

Momo reassured him, "Yes, this is the most famous and trusted information guild out there. It might look shabby and unsightly and also kind of scary from the outside, but that's just for disguise. What's important is inside. An information guild without disguise wouldn't last very long."

As Arthur and Momo ventured further into the guild through a narrow and dark tunnel, Arthur's thoughts continued to race. Momo, on the other hand, remained strangely composed.

"Why does Momo seem to be acting like it's normal for her? Shouldn't she be scared? Sigh! I have no idea what's going on here. I'm not going to be trapped here, am I?" Arthur pondered.

Eventually, they arrived at a massive door, and Momo announced, "Here we are, and I can only take you this far. Behind this gate, you will find out what you are looking for."

Arthur contemplated his next steps, "Thanks, old man."

Cautious, Arthur prepared himself for anything that might come his way. *"Now, the moment of truth. Is it a trap or something else?"*

Momo encouraged him, "Lord, you seem worried. Is there something wrong?"

Arthur put on a brave face, assuring Momo, "Haha, no, nothing's wrong, Momo. Now, shall we enter?"

As the heavy door creaked open, Arthur and Momo stepped into an unexpected sight—a place starkly different from the violent world outside, where people often clashed over even the smallest of differences. Here, the air was filled with laughter and warmth, and creatures of all kinds, races, and origins mingled freely, setting aside the barriers that defined their societies. Beasts, elves, dwarves, demons, and humans alike were seated side-by-side, sharing drinks, stories, and hearty laughter. It was as if they had all chosen to leave their pasts and conflicts at the door.

Arthur marvelled at the camaraderie unfolding before him. It seemed like a scene out of a fairy tale, a place where former rivals found solace in each other's company, enjoying the night without fear or resentment. There were, of course, occasional drunken arguments and the rare scuffle, but these were quickly diffused, and the harmony returned.

Amidst the chatter and clinking of glasses, one figure stood out—a bartender whose skilful flair for mixing drinks and performing tricks captivated everyone. He was a mystery wrapped in charm, his movements fluid and mesmerizing, as if every gesture were a piece of an intricate performance. He served drinks with a playful, flirtatious smile, but his presence radiated power and control, suggesting he was far more than just a bartender.

Arthur couldn't help but be astonished. "Whoa! What the hell is this place? Dwarves? Demons? And... wait—is that an Elf?" He couldn't stop his gaze from following a passing, enchantingly beautiful Elf, her silver hair catching the light, and his eyes grew wide with admiration.

"Ahh...! L-Lord?" Momo stammered, noticing Arthur's distracted gaze.

"Ahem!" He tore his eyes away, clearing his throat. "Right, sorry. I got a little... sidetracked." He scanned the room, focusing on the mix of races. "So, there are Elves, Humans—some of them mages—and even a few swordsmen in the crowd who don't look like they'd back down from a fight. But why is this place packed with so many powerful people, and how are they all getting along so well?"

Momo smiled knowingly. "Everyone here has something they need, something they're seeking," she explained. "Some are outcasts, some are looking for work or information, and others are just trying to escape their pasts. In a place like this, people set aside differences to find what they're missing, even if just for a while."

Arthur nodded slowly, taking in her words. "So, it's kind of like a sanctuary for the broken, a place where no one's background matters as long as they don't disrupt the peace."

"Exactly," she replied, gesturing subtly towards the counter. "But we're here for a purpose. See that bartender? Give him this." She handed him a thin, gold card marked with a five-star symbol encircled by the word 'VIP.'

Arthur stared at the card, his eyebrows raising in surprise. "A VIP card? How did you get something like this?"

Momo glanced away, a hint of mystery in her eyes. "It's a long story, and I promise I'll explain everything later. Right now, you should go. I'll wait here."

Arthur studied her for a moment, still curious. "Fine, but don't forget—you owe me an explanation."

"Yes," she replied, her tone firm but gentle.

Following Momo's instructions, Arthur approached the counter, holding up the gold VIP card. The bartender's playful expression shifted to one of respect, and he nodded, gesturing for Arthur to follow. They weaved past the tables, through a hidden door behind the bar, and down a short, dimly lit hallway until they reached a luxuriously furnished VIP lounge.

"Wait here," the bartender instructed before leaving.

As Arthur took in the lavish decor—richly coloured tapestries, plush chairs, and a faint, pleasant scent of incense—the bartender returned, this time carrying a sleek, black card embedded with a glass orb protruding on either side.

"Here," the bartender said, holding out the card. "This is what you came for. Take it and don't lose it, because there won't be a second chance."

Arthur took the card, studying its odd design. "This is it?" he asked, unsure. "But... I came here to gather information—"

The bartender cut him off with a knowing smile. "Just release your magic into the card while focusing on what you want to know. It will reveal the information you seek. But be careful—it's a one-time use. Once you use it, the card will disintegrate."

Arthur nodded slowly, pocketing the card. "Alright, thank you for everything."

The bartender waved off his gratitude with a smirk. "Huh? Thanking me? I'm just doing my job, kid. Now, off you go."

Before Arthur could respond, the bartender pressed a hidden button on the wall. The floor beneath him gave way with a sudden click.

"Wha—?!" Arthur barely managed to gasp as he was suddenly dropped through a hidden chute. He shouted in confusion as he tumbled down, sliding wildly through a dark tunnel.

A Few Moments Later...

After a stomach-churning descent, Arthur finally emerged, unceremoniously sliding out of the chute and landing with a heavy thud in an unfamiliar alleyway. He groaned, disoriented, and pushed himself to his feet, only to find Momo waiting with a calm smile.

"Whew! That was one hell of a roller coaster ride," he muttered, still dizzy from the fall. "What the hell was that anyway?"

"Oh, Lord Arthur, welcome back!" Momo greeted him with a grin. "So... how was your trip? Did you get what we came for?"

Arthur sighed, dusting himself off. "Don't even ask." He held up the black intel card as proof, then tucked it away. "We'll talk about it later. Let's get to the inn before sunset; I'm in no mood for any more surprises today."

Momo chuckled, taking the lead. "Right this way, my lord."

As they walked through the crowded streets, Arthur glanced back at the hidden entrance, still baffled by the bizarre experience but intrigued by the mysteries it promised to uncover.

At the Plum Blossom Inn

The inn had a warm, rustic charm with wooden beams lining the ceiling, casting soft shadows in the dim evening light. The innkeeper, a grizzled older man with a friendly smile, looked up as Arthur and Momo approached the counter.

"Hello, how may I help you?" he asked, his eyes twinkling as he took in the unlikely pair.

Arthur nodded politely. "We'd like to stay here tonight. Do you have rooms available?"

The innkeeper tilted his head, eyeing them with a hint of mischief. "Yes, we do. How many would you like—two rooms or one?"

Arthur opened his mouth to reply, "Hmm... Tw—"

But Momo cut in quickly, leaning forward with a pout. "One room, please," she said, glancing at Arthur meaningfully.

Arthur turned to her in surprise. "One room? Are you sure? You can have a separate room if you want. Don't you want a little privacy?"

She shook her head, her tone leaving no room for argument. "No, I want to be by your side no matter what."

Arthur blinked, trying to hide his confusion. "Ehh?!"

The innkeeper chuckled knowingly. "Ehehehe, young love these days..."

"Ouch!" Momo muttered as he playfully bopped Momo on the head. She rubbed her head with a small grin, unfazed.

"All right then," Arthur said, sighing as he turned back to the innkeeper. "We'll take a single room."

"Perfect," the innkeeper replied, handing him a small iron key with the number engraved on it. "Room 404, up the stairs and to the left."

In Room 404

As they stepped into the room, Momo froze in place, her gaze fixed on the lone bed in the middle of the room. The room was cosy but modest, with a single window overlooking the bustling street below, a worn armchair in one corner, and only one bed.

"What the... hell?" Momo muttered, her cheeks flushing. "Why is there only one bed?"

Arthur rolled his eyes, folding his arms with an exasperated sigh. "You were the one who insisted on a single room, remember? Why are you surprised now?"

She crossed her arms and pouted, glancing away. "Hmph! I just thought there might be two beds, that's all."

Arthur sighed, taking a seat on the edge of the bed and patting the space beside him. "Well, now that we're here, let's get down to business. Back at the guild, you mentioned you'd explain everything later. Well... it's later."

Momo's playful expression faded, replaced by a look of seriousness. She took a deep breath, gathering her thoughts, before sitting next to him.

"All right," she began, her voice tinged with sadness. "It's a long story... It all started when my village was raided. They looked like knights, but they weren't part of any army I'd seen before. They attacked without warning. The adventurers from the guild tried to defend us, but they were overwhelmed. Those who resisted were killed, and the rest of us... were captured."

Arthur's gaze softened. "Captured?"

"Yes," she said, her voice low. "I was out on a herb-collecting quest for the adventure guild when it happened. By the time I returned, the village was destroyed. My parents were missing... probably taken with the others. I tried to find them, but the raiders caught me. They offered me a choice: resist and die there, or surrender and go with them."

She paused, her hands gripping the edge of the bed tightly as she relived the memories. "I couldn't let myself die without knowing what happened to my family. So... I surrendered. They took me to a slave house, crammed with more than a hundred people, but I never saw my parents there."

Arthur listened, each word hitting him with the weight of her suffering. "That's... terrible."

"It didn't stop there," she continued. "We were forced into training, made to fight against the empire itself in some twisted campaign. They wanted us to fight their wars. Those who survived were either killed or sold off to slave traders afterwards. I... was one of the unlucky ones sold to a noble."

Arthur clenched his fists, anger and sorrow mixing within him. "How did you escape?"

Momo managed a small smile, though it was laced with bitterness. "One night, while the noble was distracted, I slipped away. I had no one, and nowhere to go. I lived on the streets, stealing what I could to survive. Then, one day, someone approached me, offering me a way out. They took me to the information guild, asked me to gather information, and paid me according to what I found."

She shook her head. "For a while, it worked. But then, one day, the noble I'd escaped from spotted me. My cover was blown, and the guild expelled me. I ended up back on the streets, I lived in the streets with what little savings I had left after I ran out of them only the hard-earned fifth-class VIP card I had left which I had kept for absolute emergencies."

Arthur took a deep breath, absorbing everything. "So that's why you seemed so familiar with everything back there, how you moved around without fear."

Momo nodded, looking down. "I'm sorry I didn't tell you sooner. It's not exactly the type of story you want to share right away."

Arthur placed a reassuring hand on her shoulder. "Don't worry about it. You did what you had to do. If I were in your position, I'd probably have done the same."

A faint smile touched her lips. "Thank you, Arthur."

They sat in comfortable silence for a moment until the distant chime of a bell rang through the night air, signalling midnight.

Arthur yawned, stretching his arms. "That's the midnight bell. It's getting late. We should get some rest; tomorrow's going to be a busy day. We might have to search an entire city to find that guy."

Momo looked away, blushing slightly. "Okay."

He leaned back, patting the bed beside him with a wry smile. "And don't get any ideas. I don't plan on giving up the bed."

With a small laugh, she found herself at ease despite everything, lying down on the floor next to him with a blanket Arthur had pulled from the closet. The two lay there, side by side, each lost in their thoughts but bound by the quiet understanding they now shared.

Name: Momo
Age: 16
Weight:42 kg
Height: 5'6"
Constellation: Libra
Personality: Compassionate, strong-willed, protective
Likes: Reading, martial arts, nature, friends
Dislikes: Cruelty, oppression, violence, selfishness
Dreams: Freedom, justice, martial arts mastery
Relationship: Arthur's loyal ally, bodyguard, subordinate
Skills: Martial arts, scouting, spying, assassination

Jobs: Guild's spy, Arthur's escort, assassin
Special Trait: Empathetic

43

CHAPTER FOUR

THE HUNT BEGINS

The dimly lit room buzzed with murmurs as members of the Crow Guild, cloaked in black and red, gathered around their leader, Francis. Standing at the head of the room, his eyes flashed with a calculating gleam as he assessed his loyal followers.

"Has everyone gathered here?" Francis inquired, his voice low and resolute.

"Yes, Lord Francis," confirmed Red, his most trusted lieutenant.

"Good," Francis said, steeling himself. "Let's begin the briefing. Red, go ahead."

Red stepped forward, addressing the group with a steady voice that held the weight of their mission. "You all know why we've gathered here, but for those of you new to our ranks, let me make it clear: we're here to restore our lord's rightful claim. The old fools on the council have wrongly granted the throne to the 2nd prince—an insult we cannot allow to stand. For the good of the kingdom, we will eliminate those twelve council members. And remember, this must be done covertly; no one should suspect our lord's involvement. Are you all prepared to fight for our cause?"

A unified "YES!" rang through the room, each voice charged with loyalty and determination.

Francis's gaze swept across them, his lips curling into a slight smile. "Excellent. Tonight, we eliminated the last council member. Let's go over the plan once more to ensure there are no mistakes."

He began assigning tasks to each squad with precision.

"Squad 1," Francis commanded, "you're in charge of patrolling the area. Make sure no one's in the vicinity during the assassination. No witnesses, no followers. Understood?"

"Yes, sir," Squad 1 replied, their resolve evident.

"Squad 2," Francis continued, "you'll gain access, observe, and gather all information on the target. I want every detail accounted for—leave nothing to chance."

"Understood, sir," Squad 2 confirmed.

"Squad 3, you're the strike force," Francis said, his tone harder. "Only the squad leader will approach the target; the rest provide backup if needed. This mission relies on precision."

"Understood," Squad 3 affirmed.

"Lastly, Squad 4, you'll handle the retreat and cleanup. Leave no trace of our presence. Every clue, every bloodstain—wipe it all clean."

With his final command, he cast one last glance around the room. "All right, disperse."

With quiet efficiency, the assassins moved out, vanishing like shadows, each fully aware of the gravity of their mission.

The Royal District of Hellberg, normally a haven for the kingdom's elite, rested under a shroud of silence. Nestled at the northeastern edge of the kingdom, near the royal castle, it was the safest and most guarded sector, with entry limited to nobles and those with explicit permission. But tonight, it would be anything but peaceful.

In the shadows, Red activated a magical orb that glowed a muted green as he initiated communication with Squad 1. "Squad 1, report. Is the area clear?"

A moment later, the reply came through the gemstone. "All clear, sir. We're maintaining surveillance."

"Good," Red replied, satisfied. "Signal Squad 2 to enter the 12th council member's residence and begin intelligence gathering. Report any findings directly to me."

Red launched a green flare into the night sky, a faint signal visible only to his team. At his command, the squads sprang into action, moving like silent phantoms across rooftops, scaling poles and walls, their movements seamless and practised.

"Hold here," Red whispered as they reached the edge of the council member's expansive estate. He handed each member a small communication gemstone. "These stones have a shorter range than the orb but will do for close coordination. Two of you head southeast, two northeast, and the rest follow me."

They took in the sight of the manor below—an extravagant mansion spread over a full acre of manicured land. Illuminated by countless light orbs and lanterns, the estate looked more like a place of celebration than the setting for an assassination.

Meanwhile on the Northeast Side of the Manor

"Man, this council member must be rich," one of the assassins muttered, eyeing the opulent lighting and lavish surroundings.

"Yeah, but it works in our favour," replied his partner. "The larger the place, the more entrances there are. Easier to slip in and out."

They silently entered through a rooftop window, slipping into the shadowed interior of the mansion.

"Boss, we're inside," one reported softly through the gemstone.

"Good," came Red's response. "Find the target's location and report back. Be on high alert—any unexpected activity, and you report immediately."

"Understood." voice affirmed

In Northwest Side of the Manor,

"Look, the lights are still on over here," one of the assassins whispered, nodding toward the large windows.

"Should we inform the boss?" his partner asked.

"Not yet. Let's take a closer look first. You know how he is—he'll chew us out if we report too soon." They crept closer, positioning themselves in a tree near a window. But as they peered inside, their eyes went wide with shock.

They saw the councilman—an elderly man—engaged in a lewd scene with three women on a table. His behaviour was so bizarrely intense that the assassins nearly lost their balance from sheer disbelief.

"Bro, what... what should we do?" whispered one of the assassins, horrified and repulsed. "Do we tell the boss or just look away?"

"Are you insane? Who wants to watch this crap?" the other replied, nearly gagging. "I'm going to have nightmares. Let's report back, but let's leave out the details. Let the boss get a surprise for once."

His partner smirked, holding back laughter. "Fine, fine. Hurry up; I can't stand looking at this guy anymore."

Meanwhile at the South Front Side

"Boss, target located on the northwest side," one of the assassins whispered through the gemstone. "Awaiting orders."

"Good work. What's the target's current situation? Any guards nearby?" Red asked.

The assassin hesitated. "Uh... it's complicated, sir. It might be best if you see for yourself."

"Is something wrong? Speak clearly—don't tell me you've been compromised?"

"No, sir. It's just... difficult to explain. Even if I tried, you wouldn't believe it."

Red frowned, signalling to his team. "Fine. We're coming to your location. Be on high alert; this could be a trap."

A Few Minutes Later,

Red and his team arrived at the tree, where the first two assassins were still pale from what they had witnessed.

"All right, what's the situation?" Red demanded. "This better not be some sort of joke."

One of the assassins motioned toward the window, face red with embarrassment. "Uh... just... look."

Red peered inside, and his eyes widened at the sight. The elderly councilman was indeed the target, but he was engaged in a rather compromising position with the three women.

"What in the... Are you serious?" Red growled, turning away in disgust. "You called me over to witness this?"

The assassin shook his head vehemently. "Sir, he's the target, but... well, as you can see..."

Red sighed, rubbing his temples. "Fine. I'll report this to Sir Francis. You all return to your positions."

Back at the Crow Guild, Red relayed the update to Francis.

"Sir, the target has been located. Oddly enough, there are no guards or security to speak of. It's... quite unusual, sir."

Francis frowned, sensing a potential complication. "No guards? A councilman's estate isn't exactly a tavern. Why on earth would he leave himself unprotected?"

"Well, sir..." Red paused, choosing his words carefully. "The target seems to be... otherwise occupied."

Francis raised an eyebrow, catching on. "Occupied? Forget it. Whatever keeps him distracted works in our favour. Complete the mission and leave no trace."

"Yes, sir," Red replied, his tone clipped. He activated his communication gemstone once more, signalling Squad 3. "Squad 3, commence the assassination. The target is on the northwest side. Move cautiously; if anything seems off, retreat immediately."

The scene shifts to the Northwest Side of the Council Member's Manor,

Squad 3 crept up to the window, one assassin quietly muttering, "Ugh. What a mess. I can't believe we have to kill him while he's... like this."

Their leader glanced back, his expression grim. "Just do it. Focus on the mission."

With a swift, silent command, he activated *Shadow Walk*, his form becoming one with the darkness. He slipped into the room, approaching the councilman.

A gasp escaped one of the women. "Who are you? How did you—"

"Your concern won't matter for much longer," the assassin replied, his voice low and chilling. With one swift motion, he executed *Shadow Strike*, decapitating the councilman instantly. Blood spattered the room, sending the women into panicked screams.

Turning his back to them, he prepared to leave, but their screams of terror grated on his nerves. He dispatched them swiftly, ensuring there would be no witnesses.

"Sir Red, the job is done," the squad leader reported, his voice steady as he wiped his blade clean, unbothered by the blood that now stained the room.

"Good work," Red replied through the communication gemstone. "Get out of there immediately. Squad 4 is on standby for cleanup."

"Understood." The leader signalled to his team, and they swiftly exited the manor, retracing their silent steps back into the shadows of the night.

In the dim moonlight, members of Squad 4 waited under the cover of trees in the manor garden, their breaths held as they monitored for any signs of detection. Finally, the signal came through their gemstones.

"Squad 4, you're up. Sweep the area and leave no trace. It must look like nothing happened here tonight," Red instructed.

"Roger that, Sir Red," the Squad 4 leader responded, turning to his team with a nod. "Let's get to work. Start with the windows—remove any fingerprints or evidence, and make sure we're not leaving any trails."

As the team entered the manor, they methodically erased every sign of intrusion, wiping down surfaces and gathering any stray belongings left by the previous squads. They moved with the calm precision of seasoned professionals, covering up every hint of blood and disposing of any items that might indicate foul play.

The bodies of the councilman and the women were swiftly and expertly packed into a large, heavy cloth. Squad 4 members hoisted the cloth silently, planning to dispose of the remains far from the manor, in a location known only to the guild.

Meanwhile, Francis watched from a nearby rooftop, his eyes cold and calculating as he observed the final stages of the mission. He turned to Red, who had joined him.

"So, it's done?" Francis asked, his tone indifferent yet carrying an edge of satisfaction.

Red nodded, glancing down at the distant figures of Squad 4 finishing their work. "Yes, Lord Francis. The target is eliminated, and Squad 4 is ensuring there's no trace. By dawn, it will be as if he never existed."

Francis smirked, his gaze fixed on the manor below. "Perfect. The kingdom's future is one step closer to being rectified."

The two stood in silence, the weight of their plans heavy in the cool night air. Francis's gaze drifted to the royal palace in the distance, his eyes narrowing.

"This is only the beginning," he murmured, more to himself than to Red. "By the time the sun rises over Hellberg, those fools on the council will realize their mistake. And soon, the entire kingdom will know who the true ruler should be."

Red glanced at him, a glimmer of loyalty and reverence in his eyes. "We'll follow you, Lord Francis. Every one of us. No matter the cost."

Francis nodded, acknowledging Red's loyalty. "Good. Because there's more work ahead. Much more."

With a final nod, Francis turned and slipped back into the shadows, Red following closely behind him. The night reclaimed its silence, as if nothing had happened, leaving the Royal District undisturbed and none the wiser to the bloodshed that had taken place in its heart.

As dawn broke, Francis and his most trusted guild members gathered back at their headquarters, reviewing the night's success.

"Excellent work, everyone," Francis addressed them, his voice carrying both pride and satisfaction. "Each council member we've eliminated has brought us one step closer to our goal. Soon, the throne will belong to its rightful heir."

The guild members nodded, some murmuring their loyalty, others sharing glances of encouragement.

Red, standing by Francis's side, added, "We've destabilized the council's power base significantly. They'll be scrambling to understand what's happening, and that's exactly what we want. Confusion is our ally now."

Francis nodded. "The council may be suspicious, but without proof, they're powerless to act. We'll keep them guessing, keep them divided. And once they've crumbled under their doubts and fears, we'll strike."

A sense of purpose settled over the room. Each guild member knew that they were part of something larger, something that would change the future of Hellberg. The dawn of a new era seemed closer than ever, and every person in the room could feel it.

"Rest well today," Francis concluded. "Tonight, we'll start preparing our next move. The council's days are numbered."

With that, the guild members dispersed, each ready to play their part in the next step of the plan. The Crow Guild, now Hellberg's unseen hand, would continue to weave its influence, guiding the kingdom closer to the day when Francis would claim what he believed to be his rightful throne.

The next day,

JIGGLE! JIGGLE!

"Uhm... big soft marshmallows, come to Papa!" Arthur mumbled in his sleep, a drowsy grin on his face.

SQUEEZE! SQUEEZE!

"Mmm... it's too bright..." Momo stirred, slowly opening her eyes, still caught halfway between sleep and wakefulness.

BLINK! BLINK!

As her vision cleared, she noticed Arthur's hands on her chest. For a moment, confusion flickered across her face, her cheeks flushing. Arthur, still half-asleep, opened his eyes, and they stared at each other in stunned silence.

~STARE~

~STARE~

"Huh? HUH?!" Arthur jolted back, his face going crimson. "I-I'm so sorry, Momo! I didn't mean to—uh... I, uh... I have this habit of moving my hands in my sleep. Please forgive me!"

Momo's face was flushed, but she managed a small, flustered smile. "No, no, it's fine! Don't worry about it." She waved her hands in a mild panic, avoiding his gaze. "Actually... it was my fault, really, for insisting we share a room. I'm sorry."

Arthur let out a sigh, scratching the back of his head. "If you say so... But I'll make it up to you somehow. I promise."

"Uhm... don't worry about it!" Momo said, quickly getting up. "I'll just... go check if breakfast is ready." She hurried out of the room, her cheeks still warm from embarrassment.

Arthur sighed, glancing around the room. "Another day, another blunder... Guess I'd better get dressed and figure out how to make it up to her."

Later...KNOCK! KNOCK!

"Lord Arthur, breakfast is ready," Momo called through the door.

"Alright, I'll be down in a minute," Arthur replied.

He shook his head, attempting to brush off the awkwardness of the morning as he prepared himself. "This meditation practice isn't doing much for my magic power anymore. I'll have to find some other way to improve... but how?"

"Lord Arthur?" Momo called again.

"Coming! I'll figure it out later," he muttered, heading downstairs.

The scent of freshly baked bread and savoury breakfast foods filled the air as Arthur joined Momo at their table.

"So, where are we heading today?" he asked, helping himself to a plate.

Momo sipped her tea thoughtfully. "First, we'll stop by the market. Then we'll head to the spot where Ellie was attacked to investigate."

"Why the market?" She grinned, looking a little mischievous. "Because I need to buy a few things, and it's rare for me to get a chance to roam around town."

Arthur chuckled, shaking his head. "Alright, fair enough. When are we leaving?"

"Right after breakfast. Why, do you have something else planned?" He was about to respond when the quiet hum of the inn was interrupted by nearby whispers from a group of women.

"Did you hear what happened in the Royal District?" one woman whispered.

"Yes! They say the 12th council minister was found dead with his head severed, and three women were discovered with him—completely naked," another replied, her voice filled with shock.

"Just the thought of it sends chills down my spine," a third woman added.

Arthur leaned closer to Momo, his brows furrowing. "What's with all the ruckus this early in the morning?"

She listened, her expression turning serious. "The 12th council minister was assassinated last night... in a gruesome way."

"What?!" Arthur is taken aback and shaken by the news.

"Shh! Keep your voice down," Momo warned, glancing around to ensure no one was paying them too much attention.

Arthur lowered his voice, but his mind raced. "Why didn't you mention this sooner? This is a serious matter—it's bound to draw the attention of the royal family. If I'm not there, they could even suspect or frame me."

Momo placed a calming hand on his arm. "Panicking won't help. If someone wanted to frame you, they'd have done so regardless. And didn't you leave everything with Ellie? I'm sure she can handle it."

He clenched his jaw, clearly torn. "Fine. Today we'll wrap up our business quickly and head back to the castle. But something's not right. Francis arriving, Ellie getting attacked, and now this assassination? It can't all be a coincidence. Is Francis behind this, or is someone framing him to trigger a civil war?"

As they entered the bustling Town square market, a paper boy shouted from a nearby corner. "Today's hot news! The 12th council minister assassinated!"

"Hey, can I get a copy?" Arthur asked, handing the boy a few coins.

The boy grinned, passing him the newspaper.

Momo looked around, spotting various shops and stalls. "Looking for something specific?" she asked.

"Actually, yes," Arthur replied, flipping through the paper. "Do you know any shops around here that sell magical items?"

"Magical items?" Momo echoed, raising an eyebrow.

"Yes. I need something to enhance my magical power," he admitted, scanning the stalls.

"Hmm... Magical items are rare. Most of the shops here sell cheap copies or fakes. But I know just the place you're looking for." She smirked playfully. "Follow me."

In the Dark Alley, they made their way into a quiet alleyway, far from the busy market square.

"Are you sure this is the right place?" Arthur asked, his scepticism obvious as he eyed the shadowy storefront.

Momo smirked. "For you, everything looks suspicious. Just trust me and go inside."

He sighed, pushing open the door and stepping into the dimly lit shop. "Hello? Is anyone here? Why's it so dark?"

THUD! A pile of books tumbled to the floor in the back, followed by a quiet "Owie."

Arthur stepped forward. "Are you alright? Do you need help?"

A soft voice called out, "No, no, I'm fine! I'm just... a bit clumsy. I'll be right there."

After a few moments of shuffling and reorganizing, a stunning woman emerged from the back room. She had the graceful features of a High Elf—elegant, with long, pointed ears, and a figure that seemed crafted by some divine hand. She adjusted her glasses, holding a book in one hand, and smiled.

"Welcome to Ellenor's Magic Item Shop. How can I be of service?"

Arthur blinked, momentarily taken aback. "Uh... um, I... I'm sorry, but I just zoned out there for a second."

The elf chuckled softly, blushing as she adjusted her glasses again. "Well, flattery won't get you a discount."

Arthur grinned. "I wasn't trying to get a discount; just stating the truth. Anyway, I'm looking for a defensive magical item. Do you have any?"

She nodded, looking thoughtful. "Yes, we have all types of items—some that may not even exist," she said, winking.

Arthur raised an eyebrow. "How can you have items that don't exist?"

She chuckled a touch of mystery in her smile. "That's a secret! Now, what type of defence are you looking for? Magical, physical, or a combination of both?"

"Both, ideally," he replied. "How much do they cost?"

"Well," she began, leaning against the counter, "a magical defence item costs 200 gold coins, physical defence is 100, and for both types... that'll be 500 gold coins."

"Five hundred?! Are you selling magic items or looting people here?" Arthur exclaimed, baulking at the price.

"Huh? If you don't like the price, go somewhere else," she shot back, her voice firm. "These are genuine items, not cheap imitations. Magic items don't grow on trees, you know."

Arthur sighed, defeated. "Alright, I'll take an item with both magical and physical defence."

She brought out several items, laying them on the counter. "These are our best: the Medusa Shield, the Phoenix Robe, the Pittara Rings, and the Crescent Moon Dagger. Each offers dual protection, so pick carefully."

Arthur inspected the items, his mind turning over the options. He glanced at Momo. "Take your pick."

"Me?" Momo looked up in surprise. "But... shouldn't you pick one for yourself?"

"Don't worry about me," he said with a reassuring smile. "I'll be fine. Go ahead."

After a moment, she chose the Crescent Moon Dagger. "I think this suits me best. It's lightweight and easy to handle."

Arthur nodded, hiding his relief. "Good choice. Now, do you know how to use it?"

Momo smirked. "I have my fair share of combat experience."

"Perfect," he said, turning back to the elf. "I'll take the Phoenix Robe for myself."

The elf nodded, ringing up their purchases. "That'll be 1,000 gold coins."

Arthur sighed, feeling the weight of his dwindling savings. "Fine. Here."

Reluctantly, Arthur handed over the coins, feeling the sting of parting with a fortune he had painstakingly saved. As the elf counted the coins, he couldn't help but mutter under his breath, "Goodbye, savings... I worked so hard to earn you."

The elf looked up, chuckling softly. "Worry not; these items will serve you well. Quality always comes at a price." She slid the Phoenix Robe and the Crescent Moon Dagger across the counter, each item carefully wrapped in soft cloth.

As Momo took the dagger, Arthur realized they hadn't properly introduced themselves. "By the way, I don't think we caught your name."

The elf raised an eyebrow, a glimmer of amusement in her eyes. "Hmm. Isn't it polite to introduce yourself first before asking for someone else's name?"

Arthur blinked, then laughed at his oversight. "You're right. I'm Arthur, and this is my companion, Momo."

She inclined her head slightly, a gesture both elegant and practised. "Pleasure to meet you, Arthur, Momo. I am Ellenor, a High Elf from the kingdom of Alfheim."

Momo's eyes widened in surprise. "That explains the shop's name! But... why is an elf from Alfheim running a magic item shop here?"

Ellenor's expression grew slightly wistful, but she hid it behind a polite smile. "That's a story for another day. Perhaps if our paths cross again, I'll share it. Now, if you'll excuse me, I have some work to finish." With that, she gently but firmly guided them out, closing the door behind them.

Arthur and Momo exchanged glances as they stepped back into the narrow alley.

"Jeez! What's her problem?" Momo mumbled, rolling her eyes.

Arthur shrugged, a faint smile playing on his lips. "High elves are mysterious by nature, I guess. Either way, let's focus on our next stop—the place where Ellie was attacked."

Enter Caption

Name: Vianola Carwarin
Age: unknown (above 150 years)
Weight: 60 Kg

Height: 5'7"

Constellation: Sagittarius

Personality: Confident, determined, helpful, soft-hearted.

Likes: Adventure, helping others, time with friends, magical items

Dislikes: Betrayal, cruelty, inaction, ill-nature of humans

Dreams: To protect and make a positive difference

Relationship: Close with Maria and Anya, developing friendships with Elyssa, Arthur, and Momo

Skills: Combat, potion making, all weapon mastery, magical item engineering

Jobs: Magical shop owner

Special Trait: High elf, High magic aptitude

CHAPTER FIVE

The Hard Earned Battle

Arthur and Momo arrived at a quiet, nondescript alleyway, far from the bustling heart of the city. Momo checked the guild card, which glowed faintly, confirming they were in the right place.

"This is it," she said, her voice low. "The guild card directs us to trace any lingering magical residue left by whoever attacked Ellie."

Arthur frowned, glancing around the dim alley. "So... it's like tracking gunpowder traces?"

"Sort of," Momo replied. "Everything alive has some degree of magical energy, even if it's just a trace. Wherever someone goes, they leave behind a faint residue, a trail we can track. The only way to erase it is with a secret potion, but only a few people know how to make it."

Arthur nodded, his expression serious. "The information guild used something similar, didn't they?"

"Yes," Momo confirmed. "It's how we tracked people when gathering information."

"Alright, so first, we need to analyze the magical residue left on this dagger," Arthur said, handing over the dagger that had been used in Ellie's attack. "But... I'm not sure how to start analyzing it. No one exactly taught me this skill."

"Don't worry," Momo said with a reassuring smile. "I can do it. Just watch closely, and I'll teach you later."

Arthur nodded, stepping back as Momo took the dagger. She closed her eyes, holding it in her hands. After a moment of silence, her eyes began to glow faintly, illuminating the weapon. As she concentrated, three distinct trails of magical residue appeared—one in a deep crimson red, another in a bright sky blue, and a third in a dark, nearly black red.

"There," she murmured, focusing on the last trail, which pulsed with dark, ominous energy. She glanced around, her eyes scanning the area as they followed the trace. Finally, she noticed a faint glimmer of the same residue leading down a narrow alley.

Without warning, Momo took off, running after the trail.

"Momo? Where are you going?" Arthur called, rushing to keep up.

"Shh!" she hissed, throwing him a glance over her shoulder. "I found the trail—just follow me and don't make a sound. I don't want to lose it."

"Fine, fine," Arthur muttered, keeping his voice low. He followed her through winding alleys and shadowed streets, carefully tracking her every step.

After a few minutes of hurried pursuit, they found themselves near the outskirts of the slums, where buildings were cramped together, casting dark, narrow passageways.

Momo stopped, glancing around. "The trail leads into the slums and toward the refugee district," she said quietly.

Arthur's brow furrowed. "Why would someone from here attack Ellie, let alone a member of the royal family?"

Momo gave him a pointed look. "Arthur, think about it. The people here have no resources, no backing—no one even cares if they exist. That makes them perfect pawns, doesn't it? Whoever planned this attack knew that. They probably hired someone disposable, someone who wouldn't be missed."

Arthur's expression darkened, realization settling in. "So someone with influence could be using them as tools... This might be part of a bigger plot. Either someone's trying to instigate a civil war, or Francis himself could be behind this."

"Possibly," Momo agreed. "But we won't know until we follow the trail to its end."

Arthur gave her a firm nod. "You're right. Let's keep moving and see where this leads. And, Momo? Thanks. If this helps us figure out what's happening, I'll treat you to a good lunch later."

She grinned. "You'd better."

An Hour Later, They finally arrived at a decrepit Abandoned Warehouse on the edge of the slums. The building looked empty, but as they approached, Arthur noticed men patrolling the perimeter, their movements sharp and alert.

"Looks like it's heavily guarded," Momo whispered. They ducked behind some crates, observing the area from a safe distance. "It doesn't look like any official organization... more like a rogue operation."

As they watched, a carriage rolled up to the entrance, its barred windows revealing shackled figures inside. Arthur's eyes narrowed as he recognized the occupants—mostly young women, and some children, from various races. A mother clutched her daughter, her face etched with fear, while a girl with red hair and dog-like ears stared defiantly through the bars, her age close to that of Arthur and Ellie.

Rage simmered in Arthur's chest, and he clenched his fists. "They're trafficking people. I can't stand by and watch this. I'm going to destroy these scumbags!"

Momo grabbed his arm, pulling him back. "Wait! You're thinking of charging in, aren't you?"

Arthur shook her off, his eyes blazing. "What else should I do? They're operating under my rule, and they dare to do something like this!"

She held her ground, her voice low but firm. "Arthur, I get it. But look around. There are guards everywhere, and we don't know how many more are inside. They'll use those prisoners as hostages if you go in swinging without a plan."

Arthur gritted his teeth, looking away. "I can handle them."

Momo tightened her grip on his arm. "Maybe you're strong enough to take them on, but they're not. Think of the innocent people they're holding here. We need a plan to get them out safely first. Then, you can handle these criminals however you like."

Arthur took a steadying breath, her words breaking through his anger. "Alright... alright. We'll think of a plan. But after this, I'm not holding back."

"Good. Now, stay calm and follow my lead." Momo smiles back with a satisfied look on her face.

Moments Later, Near the Warehouse Entrance, Arthur began whispering incantations, his voice barely audible as he layered protective buffs on himself. "Enhance Physique Boost, Magic Boost, Greater Resistance, Invulnerability, Dominance, Steel Body, Enhanced Agility..."

One of the guards noticed Arthur murmuring to himself from a distance and whispered to his companion, his eyes widening in alarm. "What the hell? Is he still casting? Just how many buffs is he going to add?"

The other guard scoffed, shaking his head. "Pfft, so he knows a few spells. Doesn't mean we have to be afraid of him."

Just then, Arthur launched a blazing fireball, aimed straight at a watchtower. It collided with explosive force, sending shockwaves through the area.

"See that?" the nervous guard hissed, swallowing hard. "This guy's bad news!"

"Stop acting scared!" his partner snapped. "Let's deal with him together!"

Arthur finished his incantations with a grin, feeling the power coursing through him. "Stamina Boost, Limit Break, Holy Protection, Greater Luck... Phew, that should do it. Now, who's first?"

A large thug, clearly emboldened, stepped forward. "I am. You don't look so tough to me!"

Arthur's grin widened. "As you wish."

SWOOSH! DASH! With blinding speed, Arthur closed the gap, appearing in front of his opponent almost instantly. Before the thug could react, Arthur's fist connected with his jaw in a bone-cracking blow.

WHAM! CRACK! The thug was launched backwards, skidding across the ground and slamming into the wall with a sickening thud, leaving a crater where he landed. The others froze, staring in horror at the unmoving body slumped against the wall.

"M-MONSTER! RUN!" one of the men screamed, scrambling to escape.

Arthur laughed, his voice cold. "Running already? I was just getting started." He raised his hand, summoning an enormous, invisible barrier. "Infinity Wall," he commanded, creating an unbreakable wall that sealed their escape route.

Panic spread among the remaining thugs as they backed away, looking for any way out. A leader among them, his face pale but determined, raised his weapon.

"Listen up!" he shouted. "We may not stand a chance alone, but if we all attack at once, he won't be able to fend us all off. On my command—together!"

The group rallied, shouting in unison. "FOR THE BOSS!"

Arthur rolled his eyes, chuckling. "Oh, come on. You're not even making this a challenge. Well, if that's how you want it... MAGIC MISSILE."

A dozen magic circles appeared behind Arthur, glowing ominously. The thugs froze, eyes widening as the circles transformed into deadly energy balls.

PEW! PEW! PEW! PEW! The missiles launched in rapid succession, scattering across the warehouse and hitting each thug with pinpoint accuracy. Explosions erupted, the warehouse filling with smoke, flames, and the anguished cries of those caught in the blasts.

Amid the chaos, a shadowy figure emerged, stepping out of the smoke with an aura of menace, moving toward Arthur with deliberate steps.

A Few Moments Earlier, The dimly lit interior of the warehouse was filled with the heavy scent of smoke, and the stillness was interrupted by the booming chaos outside. A large, muscular man with scars covering his bald head and body stepped out of a side room, a lit cigar hanging from his mouth. His eyes, sharp and filled with irritation, narrowed as he took in the sounds of panic echoing from beyond the walls.

"What's all this noise? Can't a guy get some peace around here?" he growled, his voice thick with irritation.

A subordinate nearby turned, his face pale. "Uh, boss... there's some guy outside. He came out of nowhere and started tearing everything apart. And... there's an invisible barrier around the area—none of us can get in or out."

The boss sneered, puffing out a cloud of smoke. "Hmph. You idiots can't even handle one intruder? Fine. I'll take care of it myself, but expect a lesson afterwards." His eyes gleamed as he cracked his knuckles, summoning dark energy around his fists.

With a powerful kick, he launched himself toward the barrier, crashing through it with a force that shattered the air like glass. As he landed amidst the dust and smoke, he grinned at the scene of chaos and destruction, his expression twisted with satisfaction. His eyes fell on Arthur, the lone figure standing amidst his fallen subordinates.

"Are you the one who caused all this?"

Arthur raised an eyebrow, unfazed. "Do you see anyone else standing here? Or are you already feeling like crying?"

The man let out a deep, rumbling laugh. "You've got jokes. You won't be so cocky once I'm done with you."

Arthur shrugged. "You can try, but I'm busy. So let's skip the small talk. I'll answer one question for every hit you land. Deal?"

The boss sneered, veins pulsing in his neck as he summoned an intense aura around him. His skin steamed, shrouded in a dark, cloudy energy that pulsed with power. "Fine. But don't expect to survive the first hit. HAAAA!"

With a roar, the man charged, his aura amplifying as he moved. The ground cracked beneath his feet, and the air around him thickened with his immense pressure. Arthur's eyes narrowed in brief surprise at his speed. He barely had time to react as the boss lunged, fist raised.

"Explosion X10!" Arthur quickly cast a series of fiery explosions, creating a rapid chain of blasts to intercept the charge.

BANG! BANG! BANG!

Each blast exploded with force, but the boss dodged nimbly, weaving through the explosions as if they were nothing. The blasts seemed to barely scratch him, and with a swift, brutal punch, he broke through the final explosion.

"Is that all you've got, kid?" the boss taunted, grinning as he closed the distance between them. "This is just getting fun."

Arthur clenched his teeth, realizing he was dealing with a battle-hardened opponent. "Fine, let's try this—Inferno Storm!" He summoned a blazing wall of fire, encircling his enemy in a towering vortex.

But the man just laughed, clapping his hands with an explosion of aura that dissipated the firestorm in a single blow. "Is that supposed to impress me?"

Arthur wiped his brow, hiding his surprise. "Alright, I'll give you this much—you've got strength. But I'm not done yet."

The man laughed again, clearly relishing the fight. "Good. Show me what else you can do, kid."

The slave trader boss lunged again, faster than Arthur anticipated, his punch smashing through Arthur's hastily raised Earth Wall with ease. Arthur's defences shattered like glass, and the boss's punch landed squarely in his stomach, sending him flying into a nearby wall. He coughed up blood, clutching his side as he staggered to his feet.

"Lord Arthur!" Momo shouted from her hiding place near the warehouse entrance, fear flickering in her eyes. "Are you okay? Should I come help?"

"No!" Arthur waved her off, gritting his teeth. "Stay back! This guy's dangerous. I'll handle him—you take the others and get them to safety."

Momo hesitated but nodded, gathering the freed captives. She cast one last worried glance at Arthur before leading them toward the forest. "Be careful," she whispered.

Arthur wiped his mouth, narrowing his eyes at the boss as he approached with a mocking grin.

"You are something, sacrificing yourself for them," the boss sneered. "Now, tell me—who sent you?"

Arthur let out a long breath, summoning his remaining strength. "No one sent me. I'm here for my reasons. But enough talking—playtime's over." He raised his hand, summoning a brilliant charge of energy around his body.

"Enhance Armament X10!" Arthur's muscles surged with power, his body crackling with an electric aura as he pushed his magic to the limit.

The boss's grin faded slightly as he sensed Arthur's raw energy. "Oh? So you're finally taking me seriously."

Arthur's face hardened. "I don't care about pride or titles—I'm using what I need to end this. Let's see if you can keep up."

With a burst of speed, Arthur launched forward, the force of his movement leaving cracks in the ground.

Clash! Arthur's fist connected with the boss's jaw, sending him reeling. But the boss quickly countered, blocking Arthur's next kick with his gauntlet-covered forearm. They exchanged blows in a brutal flurry, each impact shaking the ground beneath them.

WHAM! BAM! KAPOW!

Arthur's punches landed with enough force to send shockwaves through the air, but the boss endured, countering each attack with equal ferocity. The two seemed evenly matched, neither giving an inch as they clashed in a deadly dance.

Arthur's strength was formidable, but he felt his energy waning. The strain of maintaining his heightened power drained his magic reserves rapidly, and he knew he was running out of time.

"Not bad, kid," the boss taunted, wiping a trickle of blood from his mouth. "But I can see you're tiring out. Let's see how long you can last."

Arthur gritted his teeth, refusing to back down. "Don't worry about me. Let's just finish this."

He took a steadying breath, an idea forming. *"If I only have a few minutes left, I'll make them count."*

WHAM! SLAM! Arthur delivered a crushing blow to the boss's side, forcing him back. With a flick of his wrist, he summoned the last of his mana, preparing a final, desperate attack.

Moments Before the Final Blow,

Arthur thought quickly, realizing he'd need to pull out every trick he had. *"Alright, I'll create a weapon powerful enough to finish this,"* he muttered, closing his eyes to focus. Using his earth magic, he began forming a spear of solid tungsten, compressing it tightly. "If I can lift this far enough with wind and fire magic..."

While the boss taunted and jeered, Arthur cast his magic, pushing the spear higher and higher into the atmosphere. It reached low orbit, gaining incredible speed as it free-fell back to earth, blazing hot from the friction.

Present Moment: The Final Strike,

As the spear fell, Arthur grinned, finally feeling the weight of victory within reach. He pointed up. "See that?"

The boss followed his gaze, squinting. "Huh? I don't see anything..."

"Look closer," Arthur whispered a small smirk on his face.

In the next second, a blinding light appeared, descending toward them with terrifying speed. The boss's eyes widened as he realized too late what was happening.

"Goodbye," Arthur said quietly, turning his back.

BOOM! The tungsten spear struck the ground with the force of a meteor, exploding with a blast equivalent to a small-scale nuke. The shockwave shattered the warehouse and levelled the surrounding area, leaving a massive crater where the boss had stood moments before.

Meanwhile, at Forest Edge, With Momo and the Rescued Captives

The explosion echoed through the forest, causing the ground to tremble. Momo held the frightened captives close, shielding them from the worst of the shockwave. A small girl looked up at her, eyes wide with fear.

"Big Sis Momo, what was that?" she asked, clutching Momo's hand tightly.

Momo smiled, though worry flickered in her gaze as she looked toward the warehouse. "That? That was just your 'Big Bro Arthur' doing what he does best. He'll be alright... I'm sure of it."

To be continued in Volume 2...

A Kingdom On The Brink

As tensions ripple across the Eastern Continent, Hellberg stands on the precipice of chaos. The once-stable balance of power teeters as hidden forces push the kingdom closer to civil war. Within this maelstrom of political intrigue, betrayal, and ruthless ambition, each character is propelled toward their destiny, their fates bound by secrets yet to be unveiled.

Arthur, the reluctant hero thrust into a world of shadows and schemes, finds himself torn between loyalty and justice. Each step he takes brings him closer to uncovering the forces responsible for the attack on his friend Ellie and the sinister intentions threatening the kingdom he swore to protect. As he faces allies and enemies alike, Arthur must also come to terms with his growing power and what it means to be a leader in a world where trust is a luxury he cannot afford.

Momo, who fights alongside Arthur, is more than just an ally. With a past marked by pain, survival, and resilience, her knowledge of the darker sides of the kingdom makes her a valuable companion. However, her secrets—and her connection to a world of shadows—could both aid and imperil their journey. As Momo and Arthur delve deeper into the mysteries surrounding Hellberg, their bond will be tested, revealing the depths of her loyalty and her strength.

The Shadow of Francis

In the shadows, **Francis**, the enigmatic and volatile first prince, weaves his plans. Unpredictable and ruthless, his allegiance is unclear, yet his presence sends ripples through the kingdom. Is he a mere player in the game of power or a true force of chaos? Francis's motives are as elusive as his methods, leaving Hellberg's allies and foes in a state of constant unease. As Arthur's hunt for justice deepens, he may soon find himself at odds with a prince whose ambitions know no limits.

Power Struggles and Unseen Forces

The 12 Council Members, who once held power as protectors of Hellberg, are falling one by one, targets of a lethal conspiracy. Loyalties shift as hidden factions use pawns from the kingdom's darkest corners to execute their plans. Who commands these assassins, and to what end? Is it a plot to undermine Francis, a gambit to throw Hellberg into turmoil, or the beginning of a civil war? Arthur and his allies must answer these questions quickly, for each life lost brings the kingdom closer to disaster.

What Lies Ahead

The journey so far has only hinted at the dangers awaiting Arthur and Momo. With each revelation, new questions emerge. Who orchestrates these brutal attacks, and what do they hope to gain? Can Arthur's strength, intelligence, and determination save the kingdom, or will he be drawn into the very darkness he seeks to vanquish? In the coming chapters, alliances will be tested, secrets will be exposed, and the looming threat of civil war will bring Hellberg's people to a breaking point.

Hellberg's future is as fragile as it is uncertain, and the ultimate test of loyalty, courage, and truth lies just beyond the horizon. As Arthur, Momo, and those they encounter embark on their quest, one truth becomes clear: the hunt has only just begun.